Satellites
&
Shooting Stars

A Gravity Series Novella

by Karma Rose

Satellites & Shooting Stars,
First Edition

by Karma Rose

ISBN: 978-1-7344914-5-6

First printed April, 2021

*To all of my readers, thank you for
your ongoing support. This series
wouldn't be the same without the
encouragement you provide!*

*I wish the best for all of you.
May you all find your fireworks.*

Satellites & Shooting Stars

Robert Smith,

As of writing this, we haven't known each other long. I hope it's been longer by the time you read this.

I know we've had our disagreements and misunderstandings, but don't be mistaken. You're good for Cory. He's had so few friends in his life, let alone any who would stick their neck out like you have. I can see how much he trusts you. That's good. He'll need you—sooner than later if the doctors are right.

I'm trusting him to look after my grand-babies, but I need to know he'll have someone looking out for him, too. That's where you come in. Don't let him go through this alone. Please.

Given how little he can remember, you'll need something to reference to be the friend he needs. For that, I'm leaving you my diaries. Or, an abridged version, in any case. Nothing but the most relevant pieces. A girl's got to have her privacy.

These records, alongside what little footage or audio I've converted throughout the years, should help. They may not be a perfect account, but Cory's never needed perfect from us, just our best. This'll get you by.

Please, help him. He doesn't deserve to be alone right now. He needs people he can lean on, who'll let him grieve however he needs to. It'll get scary, Robert. The closer you get to Cory—the more you'll see of what he is—the scarier he is, but he's worth it. Trust me on that.

Get comfortable. Brace yourself. Be brave.

The Lawrence family needs you.

Sincerely,
Katelyn

<u>Prologue</u>

It had been weeks now, and Robert Smith could still hardly believe it: Katelyn had passed away. The memory of arriving at Littleton's sole, worn-down church frequently plagued him. It would play at the simplest of times, etching the images deeper into his memory of the rain, the peeling paint, and his dear friend's expression upon sharing the news.

Cory had never looked so lost before, not in Robert's experience. Even freshly released from the Institute, the demon had maintained a quiet resilience. Now, however...

"Are you sure you're okay?" asked Robert again, having to remind his friend to return to the conversation at hand.

"Hm?" Cory paused, his distraction apparent. "Oh, yes, just fine, Robert. I suppose I only need a good night's rest."

"If I can help with anything, just let me know," insisted Robert, earning a tired smile from the demon. "You know, the whole family's here for you."

"Yes, I know," sighed Cory, distracted once more. His emerald gaze wandered, falling on something behind Robert. "Oh, good heavens, Leilani, candles are inedible—no matter the scent!"

Robert watched the demon hurry to stop the newest resident from sampling a bright red piece of wax. She uttered a confused protest in a foreign language before relinquishing the candle to Cory's outstretched hand. As if becoming the guardian of two children were not enough, the poor man had to keep what appeared to be an adult demoness in check.

Cory returned to the table, setting the candle down with an exhausted sigh. He nearly dropped his head into one hand, a tic Robert found worrisome. The demon was not well.

"My apologies, Robert, I fear she is still learning," muttered Cory as he stared at the candle.

"It's okay, bud, you've got a lot on your plate." Robert watched for a minute, contemplating. Should he tell Cory about Kate's instructions? There was always the chance it could do more harm than good. "Cory..."

The demon seemed barely able to meet Robert's gaze, green eyes dulled with misery. "Yes?"

Robert hesitated before he shook his head. "It...it can wait."

"Very well." Cory's eyes drifted to stare at the candle again, brow furrowed in a scowl as he lost himself in thought. He took a hesitant breath, the scars on his face twisting wrongly with his expression. "Robert, do you suppose...Did I fail her, not realizing sooner that she...?"

"No, Cory, there was no way you could've known. Kate didn't want to worry you, and that was her choice. It's not a reflection of your character," assured Robert gently. He was unsure speaking less softly was wise when his friend looked so close to shattering.

"Very well." Cory nodded absently, green eyes glistening with tears he seemed adamant not to shed. He hesitated again. "I never should have dallied with the demons."

"She knew what she was doing." It was very far from anything Robert would have agreed with, but it was too late to change, in any case. "She wanted you to have a chance to understand where you came from, to be with people like you, Cory. Kate knew how much that meant for you and she made her choice."

"Yes, only...Robert, I am uncertain I would say the trade

was in any way equitable," whispered Cory hoarsely, the effort to speak apparent. Still, his vivid green gaze was fixed on the candle he had reclaimed from Leilani. He sniffled, shaking his head and looking startled by himself. "My apologies, I fear I am not quite recovered."

"It's okay, bud, just take your—"

"Damn it all, Leilani, *please*," begged Cory, distracted once more. "Must you attempt to consume *everything* in this house? No, Kyle, best not encourage her, now give—Thank you! Now then, you three, see if you can't count the fence posts outside, go on!"

Robert smiled glumly. This family had a long road ahead. He only hoped he would help as much as Katelyn believed he could.

Chapter One:
Echoes of the Past

I need to be honest, Robert, I'm not sure where to start. It's not just the unorthodox circumstances, either. It's the Lawrence home and Littleton as a whole. Cory's life was always uncertain, but those two elements had a way of mixing...unpredictably. We'll get to that, I guess.

Starting as far back as I know makes sense, though, right? Well, I didn't come in until a bit later, but Eleanor told me enough stories to fill in the gaps. Let's see if I can do them justice.

Eleanor found Cory in the cornfields on August 9th, 1942. She said it was hot that night, at least to her. But that's all she remembers that isn't finding him. See, he wasn't alone lying in the dirt, he was being carried by an angel. They insisted they needed to find someplace safe for the tiny baby.

Well, Eleanor wasn't about to turn away an infant, not on her life. She took him in and loved him from the very first. William was another matter. He was outraged, not only about having another mouth to feed but what kind of mouth. He'd been raised with traditional values if you want to put it politely, but if you didn't?

No, I'm getting sidetracked. William was unhappy, we'll leave it at that. Through sheer stubbornness—and several hours quoting her verses—Eleanor had her way. The Lawrences gained their third son that night, Cory Charles. Eleanor wanted him to have a kind name, for such a kind-looking baby.

5

Karma Rose

The family goat, Gertrude, helped Eleanor get Cory through until he could eat something more solid than hot cereals and, oh boy, could that child eat. She used to say he'd eat the house down to its last nail if it weren't for the chickens they kept. I believe her, too.

It wasn't easy bringing up a child so different in the best of circumstances. Never mind in a white family and during such tumultuous times. William's father, Charles, made his piece about it known any chance he got, in any way he could. When Eleanor wasn't looking, Charles did everything in his power to teach Cory his place. I saw as much, and I've been told Charles was even worse when Cory was younger—before I met him.

Cory didn't have the opportunity to have much of a childhood if I'm honest. Starting young, the other kids were quick to reject him. I'm not sure how much of it was taught or just kids being cruel, but his closest friend was always his little sister, Lisa. She was glued to his side anytime she was given the chance, until Cory saw she was old enough to be missing out on the same things he had. He always encouraged her to explore the world and stand equal with her peers.

By the time I met him, he'd started to lose what features we recognize as human. He had horns, his facial structure was rearranging, his voice was already a lot like gravel in a grinder. He was tall and lanky, and his untrained social skills didn't help him much, either. No matter what he did, he couldn't help being something so other.

I adjusted. It was different, at first, but you get used to him. I know I did. I didn't mind the things that set everyone else on edge, not at first. It was always just that he looked a bit differently. That is, until he was about seventeen, and I startled him.

He'd been minding himself, reading on the back porch before he started his evening chores. It was this old almanac, and I swear it was one of the only ten books he had to read before the rest of town pooled our extras for him. He was engrossed in that almanac, though. I guess he hadn't heard me walking up. I tapped his shoulder, that was all.

Then I was screaming, but I couldn't decide which was worse: the gash in my arm or the look on his face as he bared his fangs.

"Kate?!" His green eyes were bigger than dinner plates. "Oh, no. I-I'm sorry, Kate! Hurry, inside, Mom will have something in her first aid."

It was brief, but it was enough. Beneath his quiet manners and commendable self-control, there was something even he couldn't keep reined in, not entirely. I remember how he couldn't stop apologizing, the sweet-natured farm boy I'd always known. I didn't know what had possessed him for those few seconds, but I knew it wasn't human. It used his face but it simply wasn't Cory.

Eleanor got me patched up—it wasn't as bad as all the blood made it look, thank goodness, just a couple short cuts from his claws—and we had lunch. The day got better; Cory stayed guilty. I wouldn't be surprised if some part of him is still apologizing for the mistake.

I remember, shortly after that, he got even more strict with himself. If he started to react in any way, he always clasped his hands behind his back. Just one more thing that makes Cory the man I love, honestly—the man we all love.

Robert stared at the journals on his desk. He could not quell a sense of dread when he considered opening them again. Contrarily, neglecting them stirred guilt and obligation.

He tapped his desk rhythmically, frowning as he thought it over. He had been doing everything he could to help Cory, but there was only so much he could manage without the demon's cooperation. As it was, Cory was struggling to connect with the kids, and Leilani was still a wild card.

"Not that Kate's given me much more to work with," he muttered tiredly. He was already well aware of Cory's commendable composure—and the unfortunate circumstances for its cultivation. The demon had certainly always been calm, favoring reflection over immediate action, but Robert had pieced together a timeline for how Cory had refined this trait over the years.

Now, however, Robert feared the exceedingly strict expectations the demon had of himself would prevent the natural flow of the grieving process.

Had Cory cried at all? Almost certainly, but Robert could not place seeing his friend anything more than dazed. No mourning, no tears, no discussing how Cory felt beyond shallow observation. Was he meeting his needs, or was he too busy with the kids to think of himself?

The kids—yet another problem to solve. It was hard enough for a single father to adopt, let alone a demon. Katelyn's wishes in her will helped, of course, but Robert was taking extra precautions. He was certain losing Kyle and Sarah would break Cory beyond repair. The demon valued family above all else, after all.

The phone rang. Robert glanced at the caller ID. A shiver ran down his spine. How did she *know*?

"This is Robert Smith," he answered habitually.

"That's good, I was worried I might've dialed Santa." Beth's sarcastic reply was expected, even if her scathing tone sent another shiver down Robert's spine. "I've got those papers you wanted. I hope you know how many palms I had to grease and officials I had to sweet-talk into expediting this."

Beth, sweet-talk? How? "Thank you, Beth. You're doing a good thing."

Her displeasure was immediate. "Don't remind me."

"Still, thank you."

"He's owed something by me, isn't he?" She was quiet for an uncomfortably long moment. "I'll drop off the papers tomorrow."

The line went dead before Robert had a chance to reply, never mind wonder how Beth would know where to find him. He only hoped it was at his office. It would be far less invasive—and far less concerning how she got the information.

Robert looked at the journals again, smiling weakly. "I'm doing what I can, Kate. I just hope it's enough."

~~ * ~ * ~ * ~~

I think it's important to mention I always wanted to explore the world, and some part of Cory always wanted to come with me. He denied it, buried his worldly curiosity beneath layers of rules for himself, but it was never quite deep enough for him to truly be okay with living and dying on that farm. There was always subdued dissatisfaction whenever he talked about his future.

Encouraging him to explore how he was able didn't go as well as I'd hoped, either. He didn't pursue the few opportunities available to him on his own. I made it a point to watch for them when I realized the number of chances he'd been ignoring. Just little things, tiny cracks in the windows of the world I knew he'd always wanted to peer through.

I probably should've left well enough alone, but...I wanted to see him enjoy himself, just once.

"So...what do you think?"

Cory looked up at me from the pamphlet he held in his hand. His expression was reserved, as always, but he smiled slightly for me. "A trip to the city?"

"Not just any trip—it's a big Halloween festival!" I cheered, pointing to the pamphlet with a grin.

9

His smile stayed put, but he looked saddened by my correction. "Ah, of course. Kate..."

"You've always wanted to get out, so I thought it would be a great opportunity," I explained, losing confidence in my idea. Maybe it wasn't the best? But...I thought he'd be so excited to go. "And with it being Halloween—"

"I have work, Kate," he protested quietly, handing me the pamphlet back. I took it shyly, and he continued, "I want to go with you, Kate, because you want to explore. However, I would also be content to remain here where it will be quiet."

I stared at the paper in my hand, afraid to see what sort of expression might match his words. "It wouldn't be so bad, would it? I mean, everyone's going to be in costumes anyway."

"And if anyone were to realize this is not a mask..." He gestured a clawed hand to his face with a submissive wince. He shrugged in defeat. "I have enough trouble with Richard and his ilk, I have no desire to tempt Fate for any more of it."

"Makeup has come a long way, people might think it's just —"

"Katelyn." His tone was patient as he sighed my name. His emerald green eyes were tight with worry, eyebrows pulled together in a scowl that made his usually gentle expression seem far more severe on his face. He pursed his full blue lips, considering things carefully.

I knew that look. I'd won.

"We can stay here," I relented, even though I knew what was about to happen. It'd be poor form to celebrate too early, though.

His stern scowl turned skeptical as one brow peaked slightly. "And attend your family's usual festivities?"

I nodded in feigned defeat. "Yeah. Everything apples under the sun—candied, bobbing, carved like a pumpkin."

"An event I excel at," he boasted without changing his expression. His eyes flicked from the pamphlet in my hand to my

face, scowl turning stern again. "But you loathe those things."

"Only because, if I go to the festival, I end up having to help my family run the games and stuff," I agreed with a shrug. I could see him warring with the decision even more now, eyes darting back down and up again. "And I always end up with caramel in my hair. It takes days to get out, not even starting on the apple bits under my nails—"

"Very well, then, Kate," he submitted with a patient sigh, nodding to the pamphlet with a cringe. "I will go with you to the city, I suppose, if you cannot find another chaperon."

"Chaperon?" I wrinkled my nose in distaste at the word. "I was hoping for a date?"

Cory narrowed his eyes at me, but the gesture was equal parts playful and annoyed. "My dear, a date implies neither party is blackmailed, nor concerned for their safety."

"Blackmailed?" I gasped in horror. "I didn't blackmail you!"

"Emotionally," he pointed out with a smirk that flashed the barest tip of a fang. Good. At least he wasn't mad at me. "And I would still be worried. What if someone noticed my 'makeup' never smudges? Hm? I suppose I can spend my Halloween dodging flasks of holy water?"

"Okay, okay, fine," I relented, pursing my lips back at him now. "What's your condition, then?"

"You must ask around for another chaperon," he explained with an honest shrug. "I can't justify your going into the city on such a busy night alone, regardless of the risk. However, since this is for pleasure and not work, it is your responsibility to find yourself a chaperon."

I mulled that over, asking playfully, "And if I just so happen to forget to ask around...?"

"My dear, dishonesty will get you nowhere very quickly," he warned, fighting a grin.

I squeaked at that look, recognizing when his less civil

*side was surfacing. Oh. I guess I wouldn't be going anywhere?
"Well...that's still not bad, right?"*

*"That depends if you can remain in my good graces," he
chuckled, bending down to kiss the top of my head. He brushed
past me toward the back door, on his way out for his evening
work.*

*I glared at his back indignantly, riled up quickly at the
implication. "I guess I'll just have to ask around then, mister. I
wonder what Ethan's doing?"*

*Cory's shoulders stiffened, tail curling with a violent
twitch, but he didn't turn around. "I suppose you will need to ask
him."*

*He didn't wait for a reply, hurrying out the door as fast as
he could. Despite his size, he was gone in a matter of seconds,
the door shutting firmly behind him.*

*I huffed, glaring at the pamphlet. I should've let it go
right then, but I'd gotten myself in too deep and I was too proud
to back out. I wanted him to see the city. I wanted him to know
what he'd been missing.*

*It didn't occur to me at the time I was being selfish and a
little cruel.*

~~ * ~ * ~ * ~~

Robert gaped at Cory in disbelief. "That's...There are so
many others?"

"As I understand it, their numbers are suffering to what
they once were, but yes. There were hundreds more, like...like
me." Cory seemed to still be in awe over the revelation. His gaze
drifted toward the stairs, the sound of laughter ringing out from
the second story. "I'm not alone, Robert."

The demon's wonderment was infectious. "I take it you're
adjusting well, then?"

"Hm?" Cory focused once more on his companion with a

start. "Ah. Yes, I suppose, despite the unfortunate circumstances. Leilani can be quite the handful, but...I cannot say I am ungrateful for her company, all the same."

"I know you've probably been too busy to think much about the others you mentioned, but..." Robert hesitated, hoping he could curb his excitement enough to remain polite. "What was it like? Their village? The culture? Obviously, English isn't standard, given Leilani's inexperience speaking it, but do they all speak her language or various dialects therein? Oh. I-I'm sorry, I don't mean—"

"Not at all, Robert," chuckled Cory, careful as always not to show his fangs. His expression softened. "I am quite curious, myself. Their existence seemed primitive, although magic was applied in such effective ways it made little difference in some cases. I can scarcely begin to describe how different their culture is from how I have always lived. Their language, however—

"I find it to be a graceful translation of their innate savagery, like a purring bear. The dialects were varied, although they all spoke several with little mind to it. Goodness, even Leilani is learning English far more adeptly than I could have anticipated."

Robert smiled to hear his friend's enthusiasm over the topic. "She's a quick learner, isn't she?"

Cory nodded, his smile souring slightly. "And yet, she insists on tasting everything in sight. At least she has sorted out the candles as a whole are inedible. Now, if only she could apply the same to soap, I may be able to stop hiding it from her."

An inquisitive chirp interrupted the two men, drawing their attention to the demoness standing in the living room entryway. She smiled shyly, nodding toward the stairs.

"Babies have sleep." Her accent was heavy, adding to the sense of hesitation when she spoke. "Need, ah...eat? Soon."

"Very well." Cory's smile betrayed his enjoyment of interacting with Leilani as he stood to help her in the kitchen.

"Perhaps we should see about your learning to operate the stove, eh? Now, let me see if the pantry has..."

Robert meandered toward the kitchen to watch the two demons find snacks for when the children woke up. It was endearing to see how eagerly and intuitively they crossed the language barriers separating them. Their differences were glaring, their similarities even more apparent. He smiled. If Leilani was as good for Cory as Robert suspected, everything would be just fine.

~~ * ~ * ~ * ~~

I want to defend myself and say I tried, I actually searched for a chaperon, because that would've been a good thing. And I did ask around—anyone I knew who wouldn't be available, anyway. It was a bit underhanded, but I just knew it was for a good cause. Cory deserved a chance to have a night out, right?

In any case, that's how I got myself into real hot water. We detested each other. Why would he agree to this chaperoning business? My plan was foolproof, I'd thought, because I could go to Cory and he'd go with me to the city.

But when I asked Ethan, he said yes. He looked happy about it, too, pleased that I would consider him an option. I didn't like seeing him smile. It was wrong to see something so softening and humanizing on the face of someone who'd been nothing short of a monster to me for most of our lives.

That didn't change the fact that, technically, I had my chaperon.

"What do you mean, no?"

Cory raised one brow at my tone. "You found a chaperon."

I bristled. "Yeah, Ethan. Everyone else was busy."

He shrugged. "And you have my sympathies."

"Your sympa—You're really not going to do anything?" I cocked my hip and crossed my arms, glaring up at him petulantly. It wasn't supposed to go like this!

"Kate." He stopped himself, breathing deeply as he clasped his hands behind his back. "Please understand the position I'm in. You have your chaperon, unfortunate though it may be, and I...It would be best for all involved if I remained home."

I scoffed, too upset to stop myself anymore. "You're just going to hide?"

"Yes, I am," he snapped sharply. "You've asked me to endanger myself for your frivolity, Kate, and pretend all the while I'm in danger to play into false pretenses my face is a ruse! Would that I could peel back such a distasteful mask, Miss Katelyn, but the sinew and bone beneath fare no better to appeasing human sensibilities."

Oh, good Lord, I was never going to be able to apologize enough after that. I still haven't, if you can believe it. I'm just glad I finally knew to keep quiet.

~~ * ~ * ~ * ~~

"What do you mean, they turned you away?"

Cory's eyes fell to his hands. "They claimed the show had sold out. Never mind where they scavenged the spare tickets for the patrons behind me."

Robert struggled to keep from losing his temper. First, the pediatrician's office, now this? How often did this happen without Cory's mentioning it? Did the demon even realize it himself?

Perhaps a distraction would help them both. "Well, the kids were talking about your quick thinking to save the day?"

Cory nodded, smiling ruefully. "Ah, yes, well, I am quite grateful the two of them can be so easily entertained. We found a

15

park nearby. It kept Leilani and the children busy for quite a bit longer than a film would have, as well."

"That's good." Robert's smile still felt forced. He knew he should continue with the new topic, but the very idea of Cory being mistreated in such a way seemed to lodge itself squarely in his throat, refusing to go unspoken. "Did you, erm, call to report the theater?"

The demon's face fell as he shook his head meekly. "To what end? I've no desire to dwell on it."

"But—"

"Please, Robert." The interruption was subdued in its heartfelt plea. "Let it lie."

Robert hesitated, nodding slowly. "Okay. All right, bud, if that's what you want."

Cory smiled, gratitude apparent and lingering throughout the remainder of the visit. No matter how light the conversation became, however, Robert could not shake the deepening anxiety over how his friend had been so blatantly rejected. It was something he had never even considered a possibility, let alone one he could forget and allow to go unaddressed.

As he said his final farewells to the Lawrence family, he felt his heart jitter and jump in his throat. He had barely pulled off of the farm when he was dialing his phone. Hopefully, whoever answered would not realize he was a nervous wreck.

"Thank you for calling Bowl 'n' Watch. Are you reserving a lane or a ticket?"

"I need to talk to whoever's in charge," replied Robert, aiming for stern and certain he had failed. When had he ever *needed* to assert himself like this? He cleared his throat, listening to the sound of the phone changing hands. "We're going to have a conversation, or I'm going to make this a big problem."

~~ * ~ * ~ * ~~

16

I'm too stubborn for my own good sometimes, but you'd know that by now, wouldn't you? I'd already gotten myself in deep with my plans for Halloween and I wasn't about to back down. There wasn't anyone to prove the point to, really, but I was going to prove it.

The trip wasn't...bad. It wasn't great, but it could've gone a lot worse, given the company. Still, Ethan was a gentleman. He opened my doors, let me pick the tunes for the drive into town, and he seemed to be genuinely invested in having a good time. He wasn't the angry, spiteful boy I'd always known. He was a shining example of one of the Lawrence boys: charming, polite, witty, but still humble.

Everything I love about Cory and I still don't know how I feel about that.

It didn't take long for us to find the festivities. I'd almost forgotten they were one of the reasons for the outing at all, I'd been so caught up in my mischief. Then Ethan was opening my door again, being too darn polite to possibly be the same person Littleton had come to see him as.

"You know, you're not so bad when you're not hating your brother," I commented idly. Ethan blushed, rubbing his neck shyly.

"Well, you're not so bad when you're not fawning over my brother," he replied, his compliment falling flat. His look of horror was obvious, making me snicker.

"I'd like to think that I'm great all the time," I teased him, grinning as he cringed. I bumped him with my elbow. "I'm kidding. I could never be as shamelessly proud as you, Ethan."

"Hey," he complained with a playful scowl. "I've worked hard to be this unnecessarily pompous, I'll have you know! Do you know how much I put up with from Richard?"

I winced with a nod. "It shows."

"Ouch," he chuckled, shaking his head slowly as we continued meandering through the crowd. He sighed, breath

17

turning to a puffy cloud of smoke. "Why'd you wanna come to this whole thing, anyway? It's not really worth the drive, to be honest."

"Yeah, it's not what I was expecting," I admitted with a shrug. "But I couldn't back out once I'd actually found a chaperon."

"Trying to prove a point to a certain demon?" he guessed with a wry smile that seemed more like a grin. Oh. He was actually kind of cute when he wasn't being an ass.

"I didn't expect **you** of all people to say yes!" I laughed, shaking my head incredulously. "But maybe. He told me if I couldn't find a chaperon, then he'd come with me."

"Why do you think I said yes?" He winked at me playfully, but his admittance only ruffled my feathers.

I stopped walking, glaring up at him. "Really, Ethan? That's why you said yes? To cut off your brother?"

His eyes widened in shock and he turned to face me fully. "What? No! I mean, I guess, but I just don't want you near him, is all."

"You're unbelievable," I spat angrily, moving to shove past him.

Ethan caught me by the shoulders and gripped me tightly, refusing to let me go. "No, Kate, not like that. He's dangerous! I don't want you getting hurt."

"He's less dangerous than you!" I retorted sharply.

"And when have I **ever** clawed the crap out of you?" he demanded sternly. "Huh? I might run with Richard, but it's only because he's the only person who agrees with me that Cory is dangerous. He's not human, he's an animal! He shows you his good side; do you want to know what he did to our mother because he got startled?!"

I shoved his arms off of me. "And you're any better? You might not have clawed me, but you've done a hell of a lot worse! Or don't you remember holding me for some of the things

Richard's done?!"

"He's still safer than Cory is!" he argued, frustrated that I couldn't see what he was talking about. He followed after me as I stalked off, keeping pace way too easily. Long-legged bastard. "I'm just worried about you, Kate! Why do you think I've always tried to keep an eye on you?"

"I'm fine!" I snapped at him, startling several people around us. Why was he such an ass! Just a minute ago, I thought he might actually be a human being! "I don't need you or your convoluted attempts at concern, Ethan. Especially your trying to protect me from Cory. If I need protecting from a Lawrence boy, it's you."

"What?" he scoffed, shaking his head slowly. "No, he's the one, Cory's danger—"

*"**You** are," I snapped sharply. "**You** hurt me. He's only ever done it accidentally, but you do it on purpose, over and over again! It doesn't matter why, Ethan, just that it happens."*

"Then why did you even ask me to be your damn chaperon?" he demanded in a growl. Where Cory sounded like an animal, Ethan sounded like a livid man, lip curled in a sneer and eyes narrowed angrily.

*"Because I thought you'd say no!" I told him, exasperated as I stopped to glare at him again. "I wanted to show Cory that I was serious about going, and I thought you'd say no! I wanted to go with **him**, but you had to pick now of all times to try being any kind of a decent person!"*

Ethan glowered at me, frustrated and shocked. "You were hoping for him? He's a monster, Kate. He looks like the ass-end of Satan sat on a pitchfork, and he acts like a trained dog. He doesn't even feel things like us, Kate! He's not human, it's not right!"

"He doesn't have to be."

We glared at each other for a long minute, and it was almost a relief to have his ugly attitude back. I wasn't sure how I

19

felt about his nicer side, or actually seeing a genuine smile out of him. It was plain wrong.

"Give me a chance, then," he suggested abruptly, and I couldn't stop my jaw dropping in shock. His face twisted with a sincerely earnest expression that didn't belong there. "I don't want to see him hurt you again, Kate. Give me a shot."

I laughed once, incredulous before I realized this wasn't a joke. "Wait, you're serious?"

He nodded. "Why wouldn't I be?"

"Well, because you're a little bit more than a little racist?" I offered the first thing to come to mind. Never mind the list which didn't stop growing in my mind after that.

"And here I am chaperoning you on Halloween." He shrugged. "Let's be honest, I'm speciesist."

"And you've still done some pretty crappy things to me," I pointed out readily, not sure what to think of the look on his face now. I'd never seen him with it before, not for me or anyone, but I recognized part of it from all the times Cory stared at me—right before he kissed me.

"Let me make them up to you, then. Let me show you that he doesn't deserve the pedestal everyone puts him on," he nearly begged me.

What happened to my Halloween?! "Look, Ethan, I don't —"

"No, you're right." His jaw clenched, eyes tight, as he nodded. "It's my mistake."

We never finished that conversation, even after all these years. He made a point to act solely as a chaperon from then on, keeping chitchat to a minimum. Then he took me home, walked me to my porch, and that Ethan—the third glowing Lawrence boy —never showed his face again.

~~ * ~ * ~ * ~~

"Does your sister know?"

Cory shook his head fervently. "Good heavens, no, I could never bring myself to break her heart in such a manner."

Robert nodded in understanding. "But you're sure it was Ethan? I thought Paul was the one—"

"It was Ethan." The demon's voice was strained, verging on a growl. "He admitted to arranging the shooting, to selling his knowledge of my existence. For a place in our grandfather's will and to keep me from Kate."

"...Oh." What else was there to say? Neither Robert's professional education nor training had prepared him to help someone not human, let alone the complications such a patient might have in their family. "Cory—"

"It's perfectly fine," muttered Cory, shaking his head slowly. He sighed, the weight of the world carried in his one shuddered breath. "Nothing worth worrying over, certainly. What's done is done, and Ethan knows he's no longer welcome here."

Robert nodded once, wary to trust such a drastic change in mood. Was his friend lying, putting on a brave face to push through what was no doubt a new layer to an old trauma? The longer he studied Cory's face, the more concerned Robert became. Slowly, he realized what was so out of place.

"Cory?" The demon lifted his head enough to acknowledge Robert had spoken. "When was the last time you showered, bud?"

He ran clawed fingers through his disheveled hair absently. "Mm. I cannot recall when, but it must have been recently. I'm simply busy, is all."

"That's okay to be busy, but you need to remember to meet your needs, too."

Cory chuckled once. "Feed myself, even if it is last."

Robert frowned, confused for a moment. "That can be one way to look at it."

21

"It, ah, is a demon saying." Cory smiled briefly. "To save enough of one's resources to always feed oneself, even if it must be last."

"It's a good saying."

Cory nodded. "I have certainly found it helpful. Goodness, is that the time? Forgive me, Robert, I must get supper started. You are more than welcome to join us, of course."

"I might. Make the most of the visit and all." Robert watched the demon lumber away from the kitchen table to rifle through the cupboards. Barely having time to blink, he found himself with a new companion as Leilani materialized in Cory's seat, staring at Robert expectantly. He gulped, working to quell his reactionary fear of the woman's uncannily predatory body language. "Uh, h-hi."

Her replying smile was broad and bared a vicious set of fangs, but there was an honest enthusiasm to it which eased his tension. "Hello. How? Have good?"

Robert had to pause to ponder the question. "Oh! Oh, how am I? Good, yes, I've had—*been* good. Erm, well. I've been well. And you?"

She nodded eagerly, still baring her fangs, cat-like eyes boring into his skin. Did she never stop watching? It was unnerving, giving him the feeling of being appraised as a meal. He supposed, discomfort aside, it was a positive trait. How else had she adapted so quickly to living with the Lawrence family? She must have been giving Cory the same look, right?

Robert's train of thought halted there. It was inappropriate to ask the kids for help seeing to Cory, but Leilani was another matter. Did she understand Cory was far from himself lately? Could she grasp how mental illness might work? She always exuded a primitive aura about herself—powerful, filled with wonderment, and naïve of human workings.

Maybe it was unwise to seek her as an ally.

"Leilani." Robert squashed his doubts. He needed help

looking after Cory right now. It was unimportant if she did not understand completely—he needed to try. "About Cory—"

"Not happy," she blurted, startling them both. She smiled sheepishly, trying again more calmly, "Cory has sad. You see? Have help?"

"Yes, I know, th-that's what I was wanting to talk to you about," explained Robert in surprise. How much more did she already know? "Erm, that is, I need help making sure his needs are met, that he's cleaning himself, being fed, sleeping at night—"

"Sleep?" She mulled over the word for a moment before shaking her head. "No. Has bad sleep. Small eat."

"That's what I was afraid of," he muttered with a frown. He eyed Leilani. Cory responded to her better than anyone else Robert had seen lately. It was worth a shot. "So, that's how you can help, Leilani. Help him eat, help him sleep, help him stay clean."

The demoness watched Robert for a long moment as she absorbed her instructions. She nodded, setting one hand on Robert's shoulder. "I help Cory smile. Yes?"

Robert did not have the opportunity to clarify the matter further, watching as she flitted off with unnervingly graceful movements toward where Cory worked in the kitchen. She must have understood, though, right? Then again, maybe not. Their cultures and languages were vastly different, after all.

A sound stopped Robert in his tracks, unable to continue preparing to leave—when was the last time he heard Cory laugh so genuinely?

~~ * ~ * ~ * ~~

I never told Cory what happened that Halloween. Those two brothers didn't need any extra kindling toward their animosity for one another. Jeanine, on the other hand, wanted to see Cory give Ethan what for.

23

"No, Jeanie, I'm not stirring any pots."

She sighed dramatically. "It wouldn't hurt anyone but Ethan, and that would only be a little bit!"

I rolled my eyes. "It wouldn't be fair to Cory."

"Ugh." She fell back on my bed. "He's such a softy. One little fight wouldn't hurt."

"You know that's not true." I frowned at my math pages. "I'm not sure Cory could stop if he got started."

Jeanine rolled onto her stomach, smiling for my sake. "Don't be so down. Has he ever made you question your safety with him?"

"No, but—"

"And Ethan doesn't need to," she pointed out. "We know he's a terrible person. So if Cory just gave him a tiny, teeny little love-tap to the face—"

"Jeanie, no!" I couldn't help laughing at her expression. She'd made a point. Cory was the safest person I knew. Telling him wasn't necessarily a bad idea, but...I didn't want to risk it hurting him, either. He deserved to know he was safe with me, too, right?

Setting aside the diary and its latest entry, Robert looked across his desk at the box it was originally delivered in. Curious, he inspected the contents again, rewarded with a tape player he suspected could be as old as his parents. He plugged it in before selecting one of the tapes, labeled with an aged piece of painter's tape: Session 1.

The *clack* of each button stirred nostalgia for Robert, and by the time the recording started playing over its old speaker he was giddy, grinning like a kid at Christmas.

Static, then—

"Katelyn, what is this?"

Robert's shock felt like jumping in a frozen lake to hear Cory's younger voice playing.

A giggle. *"I'm borrowing this from a cousin, and I sort of need your help to pay off the debt I owe them."*

"Oh, dear." A heavy sigh laced with static. *"What have you gotten yourself into, my dear?"*

Robert chuckled; he could only imagine the look of indignation on Kate's face. *"In exchange for us getting to play with this lovely device, he needs some recordings."*

"Recordings of...?"

The sound of the microphone shuffling was bracing. *"Well, said cousin is trying to do a radio show, but he needs some new music, so that's where you come in, mister."*

"Ah." A pause. *"Best not."*

"But—!"

"My beautiful Miss Katelyn, need I remind you how your schemes so often end?"

"I brought a fire extinguisher this time. Besides, there's no one else involved. It's just you, me, and the recorder."

"Kate..."

"Just sing with me."

"Come on, Cory," muttered Robert, cheering silently when he heard the defeated sigh of his friend.

"Very well, my dear."

"You're my favorite person."

"Mm, and if I were Achilles, you would be my heel. Now then, how does this contraption work?"

"Oh, it's been recording. So now we just—"

Robert nearly fell from his chair. He had never heard Katelyn sing, and he had to wonder if the old recording did her voice any justice. The melody lilting from the ancient player was light, with all of the spirit of the singer herself.

Then another voice joined hers, soft and steady, so far from the constant near-growl Cory was only able to speak in. If

25

the demon's casual cadence were crashing boulders, this would be the serenade of thunder itself, rolling from one word to the next with the enchantment of a storm. This voice, Robert knew, was served an injustice by the recording's quality alone.

Settling into his office chair, Robert closed his eyes to listen. They sang old hymns he did not recognize, the duet's intuitive compatibility haunting as thunder chased lightning in an audible force of nature which could never perform again. Nevertheless, he understood why the church stood still when Cory harmonized, with a singing voice from the heavens themselves to contrast the demon's hellish natural timbre.

The night passed in a trance as Robert played one tape after another, grateful for whatever good fortune kept them in working order this long. The rest had a mix of genres, from the old church hymns to swing numbers, to early rock and the odd bit of country—which Katelyn always sounded reluctant to join in on—the duets carried on. Before he realized it, the last tape *clack*ed its finishing note, leaving Robert in an unwelcome silence, unsure of what to make of the experience and desperately hoping he could preserve the recordings on something more resilient to time.

<u>Chapter Two:</u>
<u>Social Conventions</u>

But that leads me to the only time I've ever questioned my safety with him, or how deep his humanity runs.

It was Dustin's wedding. We were young: Cory was barely into his twenties. Every milestone his siblings reached always seemed to be a painful reminder for him of what he is. It's not like he could move away from the farm. No matter how badly I knew he wanted to raise a family of his own, there were too many variables, too much stacked against him.

Dustin and Anna Belle had shown up during the early afternoon, a few hours after Cory had turned in. Well, Dustin thought it would be best if he left a note on the door telling his brother about the house guest, rather than actually knocking, but I was too interested in what he had planned to step in, honestly.

You see, he and Anna Belle had just gotten engaged a few days prior, and she had started planning the wedding immediately. Dustin wanted his brother to be a part of it, though, so he insisted on taking a few days to visit the farm and his brother, so the happy couple could start thinking of a way to broach the subject with the guests from her side.

Needless to say, I've never been able to forget that experience.

I was sitting at the kitchen table with Dustin and his fiancée, waiting for Cory to join us. I would've been biting my nails if Eleanor hadn't broken me of the habit. It was coming up on four, about the time Cory usually woke up. I could hardly sit still, but Eleanor had insisted I be the one to entertain our guests while she toiled over the stove to make sure dinner was still on time.

"So, a wedding," I said stiffly, my foot tapping the floor quietly.

Dustin smiled and nodded, trying to smooth over the awkwardness. "We were thinking a spring wedding, when everything's in bloom. Weren't we, darling?"

Anna Belle nodded as well, forcing a smile as she looked me in the eye awkwardly. "Oh, yes, it's going to be beautiful."

"Right, well, congratulations! Again," I petered off, freezing when I heard the door upstairs. I wanted to jump up from my chair and give Cory a fair warning, but I heard the pause before he lumbered down the stairs. He must've seen the note.

"Sounds like Cory's awake," chirped Eleanor, and her voice gave away just how anxious she actually was. I understood then why **she** *had to be the one cooking.*

Oh, and it did sound like he was at least able to see where he was going. It was almost like a film, listening to the booming steps as he trudged down those stairs, him clasping the wall to maneuver his bulk out of the tight hallway and toward the kitchen. I was facing the hall where he was coming from, watching his slow saunter as he yawned wide and did his best to stretch in what space he had. I gave him a tight smile and he smiled back, not quite realizing who all was at the table until he was practically in the kitchen.

He jerked his head in surprise, the back of his skull cracking against the ceiling. "Oh!"

Anna Belle turned to look at him, concerned, gasping in shock. "Oh, my!"

Dustin braced himself. "Now, honey..."

"Who is she!" demanded Cory, panicked, one of his horns

lodged into the ceiling. He pulled it out forcefully, backing away in fear. I had seen him fight off gangs of the worst people in town, and he was afraid of such a little thing!

I was on my feet in an instant to help Cory calm down. Behind me, I heard more commotion and glanced back to see that Anna Belle had fainted. Cory wasn't fairing much better, tripping over his own tail and crashing to the floor. At the stove, Eleanor's strained humming could be heard over the utter ridiculousness of the situation.

~~ * ~ * ~ * ~~

"Can you believe this?"

Robert looked up from his coffee to see the morning paper his brother was reading. "What's wrong now, John?"

The paper rustled as John tossed it to the table in apparent disgust. "All this crap about demon rights. Freaking bleeding hearts think it's too much to ask the damn things to take a quick test."

Robert felt a pang of anxiety in his gut. "Erm, i-it is a little unreasonable."

"Thank you!"

"No, not—The tests, they're unreasonable," he clarified nervously. He shook his head, finding it difficult to look his brother in the eye. "It doesn't take a test to see if they're people. They're just people."

"Oh, no." John sighed, the sound laced with disappointment. "You, too, huh? What next, you're going to tell me my dog's a person, too?"

"That's not—"

"You should know better, Robby, or were you not paying attention when demons started attacking people?" John's tone grew more scathing with every word. Robert did not need to look to envision his brother's hateful sneer. "Dad would be disappointed to hear you defending those animals."

Robert took a deep breath, steeling himself as best he could as he forced himself to stare down his sibling. "Cory's not an animal, John. He's a man who's been dealt a bad hand and at every opportunity he only ever plays it compassionately."

John scoffed. "That's right, I forgot about your *patient*. I thought you were just in it to get your girls through school?"

Robert felt a stab of guilt, but he refused to crumple. "Not anymore. I met someone who changed my mind on a lot of things."

"Yeah, well, it's a real buzz-kill." John smiled tightly. "Don't bring it to breakfast next time, huh? No point to it when we should just agree to disagree."

"Erm, I guess..." Robert returned his focus to his coffee, unable to shake the budding remorse of his silent betrayal of Cory. His friend would never blame him, but likewise Robert knew the demon would always defend him.

If only Robert had an inkling of how to act with such humanity.

~~ * ~ * ~ * ~~

The visit got better. Once Cory and Anna Belle worked through the initial shock, they got along famously. Not that either of them seemed to be the chattiest, but their shared silences were friendly enough, at least. In the end, it was mostly Dustin and Eleanor talking about possible complications of what he wanted to achieve.

"...I could simply stay home." The quiet suggestion was subdued, Cory's eyes fixed on the table. "That is, it would be easiest for everyone—and safest for me—if I remained uninvolved with your wedding."

"You're kidding, right?" Dustin pat his brother on the shoulder. "I can't get married without the best man there."

The revelation was gradual for Cory while Eleanor and I felt its impact like a gut-punch. She sniffled, seconds away from a total meltdown. I grabbed her hand to help ground her, regretting it instantly when she returned my grip with bone-crushing desperation.

"Me?" wondered Cory with a frown. He shook his head. "What about Ethan?"

Dustin shrugged. "Too much drama. 'Sides, I wouldn't trust anyone else to do the job like you could."

Cory managed to keep his meticulous composure. Meanwhile, Eleanor was a blubbering mess and I wasn't too far behind. Anna Belle, bless her, swallowed her very obvious discomfort to put in her own words of encouragement.

That was the start of many, many, many more visits from the couple as they planned out the details and brought more of the bride's family to meet the best man ahead of time. Cory never adjusted, Anna Belle came by her fainting honestly, and it was a small disaster every time. We all agreed, though, that it was best to acclimate everyone slowly, before the big day.

On the other side of the stressful visits, Cory and Dustin managed to bond more over the year of planning than I'd ever seen them when they were younger. You should've seen it. That giant man finally came out of his shell a little bit, acting more like himself with every visit. He even started smiling and laughing— things he rarely did those days for fear of baring a fang.

It was during one of their visits close to the wedding when I got a little too nosy. The brothers were in their father's study for privacy, while Anna Belle and Eleanor gushed over arrangements in the living room. I'd been sent to check on them, overhearing Cory mention my name and—

"...but Katelyn deserves to make the choice, of course."

I stayed where I was, hidden behind the stairs while I listened to the two men talking quietly.

"Really, you want her to live here? Cory, that's great!"

congratulated Dustin happily, laughing. "Do you have any idea when?"

"No, not precisely," replied Cory shyly. I could just imagine him blushing at the topic. "I imagine she will want to live with me, in my room."

"You should propose."

I heard Cory choking on something. "I'm sorry?"

"You should propose to Kate," Dustin repeated himself firmly. Then explained, "Look, obviously, she's ready for commitment, Cory. What are you waiting for? You've been childhood sweethearts long enough, it's time you tied the knot."

"Oh, I'm not too sure about that. Perhaps a couple of years of living together, just to see—"

"I'm going to tell Anna Belle to throw the bouquet straight at Katelyn. Then you'll have absolutely no choice but to get married next," interrupted Dustin with a master plan, laughing at what I was sure was a priceless expression.

"Truly, Dustin, there's no need to get her hopes so high," scolded Cory. I glared at the wall. What was he talking about? I'd been waiting just a bit too long to get my hopes this high! "It's only a phase, I'm sure. Any day now, Kate will come to her senses and find a man who can solidly provide for her. In the meantime, all I can do is indulge her fantasy."

*My **fantasy**? I gritted my teeth in aggravation. Did he honestly still think I would leave him that easily? When I wanted to move in with him without being married?! Really, how obvious could a girl be without getting down on her own damn knee with a ring!*

Dustin sighed patiently, sounding sympathetic. "Cory, if you're not careful you're going to wake up one morning and she won't be there because there was no wedding and no other reason than that."

"I know," sighed Cory. "Just...Look at me, Dustin. What kind of life can I give her? Not one with travel, or friends, or

family. Not with nights on the town or parties in our own home—not children, you know that. Wouldn't it be better for her if I never committed us to that? She deserves an escape route, at the very least."

"She **deserves** *a white dress and you writing the most poetic vows mankind has ever heard," his brother argued back. "After all, you don't know about the rest of that. The world's changing, Cory, just look around. It's only a matter of time before you get your own rights, and you can make up for all of that lost time with her then. Leave this farm, go raise your kids in another city! Just remember to send postcards and visit for the holidays."*

"Very funny, Dustin."

"I'm serious! You deserve all that, too. You **both** *deserve to have the happiest marriage this world has ever known. I've seen you two, the way you look at each other. One minute—all of the love and care you two share in one minute—I don't think I've ever felt that much in my entire life combined. And* **I'm** *the one getting married," he scoffed. "You're perfect for each other, really. The sooner you see it, the better."*

Cory sighed, and I could hear the debate in that sigh. It took him a long minute to answer. "I suppose you're right, Dustin. Let Anna Belle toss Kate the bouquet, I'll arrange plans to propose."

"Better yet, little brother, why don't you use this?"

"I can't use this, Dustin! This is—"

"Take it and use it, Cory. During the reception, propose to her with that and if you really **need** *to, we can see about switching out the rings before you do. Keep it on you in the meantime, though—in case you find the perfect moment."*

Another pause. "Thank you, Dustin. Truly, this means more than you can imagine."

"Really, I'm happy to help shove you in the right direction, just as long as I get that sister-in-law I've been waiting

for."

"Perhaps we should focus on you and your own bride first?"

"I know, I know. Two more weeks and I'm a married man. Smooth sailing from here, right?"

~~ * ~ * ~ * ~~

The unassuming piece of mail on Robert's desk dominated the room with the daunting message it bore. Cory had enough worries on his plate right now without this being added. His kids had only just settled down after the excursion with their father, and his depression was still a looming force in itself. How much more could the man take?

This was something best handled face-to-face. Robert checked his watch worriedly. Still early. He had plenty of time to drive out to Littleton for a visit and still be home by dinner. The sooner the better, right?

Robert felt his heart sink. There had to be something he could do to help get Cory out of this. But if the demon refused, there was a chance Leilani could be exposed. There was too much controversy to risk it.

He grabbed his phone on impulse, flipping through his contacts with a mad urgency. Finally, he found who he was after, waiting anxiously for an answer as the call rang through. It was his only shot, really.

"I'm not even through my morning coffee, Robert, this had better be good."

"I got a letter from the Institute."

Not even a pause before, "I know."

Of course, she knew. She had to have been in on it! Who else could have possibly wanted to make Cory suffer unnecessarily?

"Beth, this has to be a joke." Robert took a deep breath to

keep himself from all-out screaming over the phone. "You can't do this to him."

"Believe me, I tried to put wrenches in the program," snapped Beth sharply. "Why do you think they've taken this long to send the damn letter in the first place? I've brought up every scrap of red tape I thought I could to stall!"

"Then..." He felt a pit in his stomach to realize this went beyond the face he had always placed on the Institute. "You're not the one pushing for this, are you?"

"The higher-ups aren't happy that Cory hasn't relapsed yet. They're getting impatient." She grumbled a sigh. "Word in the labs is that his release was all a pony show. I'd brace for things to get a lot worse for non-humans in the next few years."

He felt the blood drain from his face. "How much worse, Beth?"

"...I didn't want to know they'd never let him go. I just wanted to make sure my son got through college."

"Beth...?"

"If he cooperates, it won't be as bad for him. If he gives up the others, they might leave him be entirely." Beth sighed. "But if he stirs any pots...You document everything, Robert, do you hear me? The second it gets out of hand, you raise hell and you don't stop."

He smiled weakly. It was far from anything he had ever done before, but he would do his best for the Lawrence family. "What's your stake in this?"

She took a moment to answer. "I'm not going to repeat my mistakes, Robert."

~~ * ~ * ~ * ~~

It's Dustin's fault, really. He should've known better than to invite a jinx so close to the big day. But we finally got the RSVP Cory had been most anxious about.

"Grandfather Charles is coming? To the wedding?" asked Cory, and I could see genuine fear in his usually bright eyes. I made to hold his hand, for comfort, but he pulled away with a shaky sigh.

Eleanor's smile fell in an instant, but it was William who answered, quiet and firm. "Of course, he's coming to your brother's wedding, Cory."

"Is there any way—?"

"We've gone over this enough times, son, you will be respectful of your grandfather and I won't hear another word about it!" snapped William, startling me with his ferocity. "Am I understood?"

Cory's jaw tightened, tears in his eyes, but he nodded tersely. "Yes, sir. Excuse me, I need to get to sleep."

Without another word, he stood from the table, his plate completely untouched. Worry twisted in my gut, claiming my appetite with it. I looked to Eleanor for answers, but she just shook her head. I sighed quietly, not needing to debate very long before I stood up.

"Please, excuse me, too," I mumbled.

"No, he needs to sit with himself and how he treats his grandfather." William gestured to my place at the table. "Sit."

"But—"

"Kate, dear, I'll need your help clearing dishes in just a minute?" interrupted Eleanor with a strained smile. I know she was only trying to keep her husband from getting wound up and lashing out. She was looking out for me; it felt like a betrayal that she wasn't defending someone checking on her son.

That afternoon lingered for the days leading up to the wedding. I'd never met Charles before; Cory rarely spoke about him. There was no way for me to anticipate how bad it could get.

Before we knew it, it was time for us to get ready for the ceremony. Cory had gone to the church early, while it was still dark to avoid unwanted attention. The rest of us were too busy to *join him until later and I couldn't shake my jitters. Something about that morning plain didn't feel right.*

Jeanine was about done with my nonsense by the time we arrived at the little old church. "Katie, I know you're in a mood, but if you keep this up I'm going to be in a mood."

"You should've seen him the other day, Jeanie," I fussed. "Ooh, and that's not to start on the fact the bride's entire family could faint from shock if there's so much as a breeze."

She cackled. "What I wouldn't give to see that!"

For such a small building, it held a surprising amount of people all trying to find their seats. Most of the signs on the pews had been covered with flowers, except for one in the far back. At least we knew where we were sitting. Now, if only I could figure out where—

"Oh, honey," cooed Jeanine, tapping me on the shoulder and pointing out where Cory was standing down the aisle from us.

I stopped there, unable to help staring. Cory was absolutely breathtaking, six eleven high and nearly half as broad in his trimly cut suit. I remember watching him tailor that suit, but I never thought he would be so handsome. His natural grace was accentuated cleanly, his rich red tones stark against the black of his jacket. Where his midnight-black hair would have framed his face was empty, trimmed down and combed neatly, giving his squared jaw and otherworldly face such a professional aura I could hardly believe he was the same man. My heart leaped a little in my chest, making me smile.

"Go on, enjoy time with your Prince Charming," sighed Jeanine, giving me a teasing smirk. I nodded.

Cory looked over then, smiling at me. My heart leaped again at that. He waved me over, turning back to the older man he was speaking with. Little did I know, I was about to meet Charles Lawrence.

In a matter of seconds, I realized why Cory had reacted

that way; why Eleanor was desperate to keep the situation from devolving more than she knew it would; why William was such a spiteful creature about the topic.

In a matter of seconds, I realized a real demon was attending the ceremony, and my disappointment that the holy ground he walked on didn't burn him cut deep.

In a matter of seconds, I wanted to forget I'd ever met the monster named Charles.

~~ * ~ * ~ * ~~

Robert knew he would have nightmares of this for years to come, watching the fight drain from Cory's eyes. He was no longer the proud man Robert had befriended, but the husk of a broken animal, wounded and whimpering as it limped in its cage. Cory's lips moved as if chanting to himself. Robert could only wonder if the words were a mantra or a reminder of the woman at home, defenseless in light of the newest laws passed.

The bone saw whirred to life; the demon flinched at the sound. As it bit into his horn he grimaced, face warped from fear. His blood flew across the attendants' smock and gloves, running down his horn, into his hair, and across his brow. He pinched his eyes shut tightly, reciting his reminders more furiously than before.

"It's good to know he still behaves well in the chair," commented one of the attendants. Robert grimaced, listening to his friend's low protests as a backdrop to the praise of the demon's assailants. Did they not realize what they were *doing*?

"AH!" Cory tensed, hands gripping the chair for dear life as his eyes flew open and every muscle across his frame coiled for a fight. He gasped sharply, winding his tail around his leg and clenching his jaw to hide his fangs. Tears mingled with the blood on his face.

"It's just a nerve," explained the one with the saw, no

doubt noticing Robert's immediate horror. They shrugged. "He won't hurt you. It's a pretty normal reaction for this sample collection."

"Normal?" echoed Robert. He shook his head slowly, a hundred ways to scold such callousness catching on his tongue. He could not open his mouth to speak them, choking on the disappointment of his fellow humans as much as the disappointment he held for himself. All these years, Cory had deserved better. All the years to come, and it seemed as though each step for demon rights were going backward.

"Huh, that's new."

Robert forced himself to focus, noticing the interest one of the attendants had taken with the bracelets Cory's children made for good luck. He explained their origin, adding submissively, "They don't even know he's here."

"My kids make me stuff like that, too," laughed the attendant, humor falling short as they realized their words. They cleared their throat nervously. "C'mon, let's get this over with."

Still, Cory mouthed his reasons to himself urgently, barely present for what was to come as they set aside the saw and reached instead for a pair of forceps.

~~ * ~ * ~ * ~~

To my relief, the ceremony blurred by, and Charles kept his hateful self far away from the "riffraff"—me, Jeanie, and Cory in particular. I guess he'd fulfilled his obligations of cruelty for the day. I wasn't one to look a gift horse in the mouth, and I didn't go looking for reasons he kept his distance. That he made my avoiding him easier was mercy enough.

To my frustration, though, it seemed Cory was avoiding me, too. He kept finding ways to slip away from me, barely ever saying a word when I found him again. Infuriating as it was, I couldn't help being more worried than anything. Had Charles said or done something to Cory when I wasn't looking? Sad as it was that my own man wouldn't dance with me at the reception, I couldn't shake my nagging concern.

"What are you so worried about, Kate?" laughed Jeanine, not taking my concern seriously. "The entire wedding, Cory's eyes weren't on the bride and groom, I can tell you that."

*"How would you know that?" I wondered for a second, shaking the thought from my head. "You know what? I don't need to know. Ugh, where **is** he?"*

"How do you lose a seven-foot red man?" she countered, finishing her glass of champagne. She tapped me on the shoulder, pointing across the floor to a dark corner. "Is that the Lawrence you're looking for?"

I spotted him in the shadows and breathed a sigh of relief, smiling and waving to him across the room. He straightened abruptly, the room still too dark for me to clearly make out his features. I watched him link his hands behind his back, turning away from the dancing and going straight for the exit. I frowned, worry and rejection propelling me through the crowd to catch Cory before he escaped.

He had already made it out the door and was a solid thirty feet from the building before I was even off the porch steps. My heel caught and tripped me, but I forced myself back up to call after him, "Cory, wait!"

He stopped where he was, hands still firmly clasped behind him. "What is it, Miss Katelyn?"

"What's going on with you, Cory?" I asked concernedly, limping to close the distance between us.

Cory sighed quietly, tail whipping the air abruptly. "Nothing you need concern yourself with any longer, Katelyn. Have a pleasant evening."

"No, wait—Cory, wait!" But it wasn't any use. He was off and flying faster than I could ever hope to catch him. Jeanine showed up beside me, a fresh glass of champagne in hand.

"Wow, he's..." She struggled to find the word for a minute. *"Tense."*

I stared at her, unamused. *"Now's when I'd like some advice, Jeanie, not commentary."*

She shrugged. *"Enjoy the free alcohol? Otherwise, I got nothin'. A week ago, he was happy as a clam. Now he's in a mood. I figure you'd know."*

In hindsight, Jeanine's suggestion was better than my bright idea of chasing after Cory; I followed him back to the Lawrence house anyway. I didn't even know what I was going to say, only that I wanted to get to the bottom of whatever was eating him.

When I got there, the house wasn't lit up, given everyone else was still at the reception. Cory never needed the extra lights, but he always used them. I guess it was a habit from living with people who did need them.

Trying to find him usually wasn't that difficult. He's a seven-foot crimson Goliath with wings! I still blame it on my shoes—heels are difficult enough without hiking across fields, y'know? But I found him, finally, at that old tree in the back. We'd spent countless happy, sunny summer afternoons under its branches. It was a stark contrast to the chilly, moonless night, and the weight of the atmosphere as I approached.

There was a breeze, shifting to put him downwind of me. He looked up, alert. It always reminded me of a dog, how sensitive he was to his surroundings. He'd told me before he enjoyed how I smelled. I only hoped I wasn't the rabbit to his dog in this scenario.

"Katelyn." His expression hardened. *"I thought I made my desires for the evening clear?"*

I crossed my arms and cocked my hip. *"Not really, mister, you've been too busy avoiding me all day."*

"With good reason," he muttered bitterly, shaking his head slowly. *"It would be best for us both if you would leave,*

41

Miss Katelyn."

"Excuse me?" I raised one brow, scoffing. "No, it would not, Charles, not before you talk to me and tell me what's wrong!"

"Must you be so dense?" he seethed. He stood smoothly, stalking forward a few steps. He wasn't making an effort to restrain himself; every movement made me think I was definitely the rabbit here. Then he bared his fangs in a sneer. "I have no desire to associate with you, now or in the future. My grandfather has reminded me quite plainly of the importance of keeping to my own breed."

"And what the hell does that—!"

"Leave me be!" he roared. Something visceral—a sound gut-wrenching and inhuman—slid between his fangs, echoing back across the fields behind me.

I froze, locked in place even though my legs screamed for me to run. I couldn't move, though. He looked too much like a monster and I didn't want to risk him giving chase.

My reaction isn't something I'm proud of. You need to understand, we'd gotten so used to Cory being tempered, mild, synonymous with safe, I had trouble remembering he was still...whatever he is. Still not human. There are parts of him that, when he lets them show, it's like staring down an angry bear, but a hundred times worse. I could try to scare off a bear.

When Cory showed those parts he's so good at hiding, I thought there was no saving myself. He could tear me limb from limb, and I wondered if some part of him would enjoy it. I know it's not his fault, what he is, and it's not even **who** *he is by any means.*

None of that justifies what I did.

Cory growled. He sounded like a rabid panther. "Well?!"

I screamed. It was blood-curdling and strained my throat so badly I would be coughing on the taste of copper for a week. I stumbled, tripping out of my heels as I fled for my life from the

*unnatural thing possessing Cory. I didn't stop at the road, just
wanting to make it home no matter how badly my lungs burned or
deeply bruised my feet felt.*

*All I knew was I needed to get away because whatever I'd
followed to the back fields that night wasn't my Cory.*

~~ * ~ * ~ * ~~

It could have been worse, Robert reminded himself
sternly. He had started the day anticipating it going much, much
worse. It could still get worse.

They had made it back to the farm. Robert's preparations
made the transition easier, he thought, but Cory's arrival home
had been too much for the demon's frayed nerves and fractured
composure. Still, it could have been worse—much worse than
Lisa taking the kids for a weekend, worse than Cory's family
being startled by the toll the day had taken on his already-strained
psyche.

Robert reminded himself again as Leilani finally returned
to the living room from her venture upstairs. Had she even
managed to get into Cory's room? The door was barricaded when
Robert tried to check on things. He doubted the demoness's
efforts fared much better.

Regardless, he could not quash his curiosity.

"Leilani..." Robert threw a furtive glance over his
shoulder, toward the stairs. "How was he, while you were up
there?"

The coral demoness hesitated, cat-like eyes flicking to
follow his gaze. "Has sad. Has hurt. Why?"

The question caught Robert off-guard. He had grown
accustomed to those around Cory knowing his friend's
circumstances. Faced with the challenge of explaining such a
gruesome history, even in its barest form, Robert was uncertain he
could rise to the occasion.

Leilani's copper eyes begged for an answer and a way to help the broken man upstairs.

"He, erm...He met some bad people, and they used him to satisfy their curiosity." Robert forced himself to meet her gaze no matter how painfully inadequate he felt in the moment. "They caged him for a long, long time, because...because people didn't want him outside, until recently."

How much did the demoness understand? Robert knew she was still learning to speak English, except... From the gleam in her eye, he wondered how observant she truly was. He felt as though she could see straight to his own guilt in keeping Cory locked away longer than he should have been.

She smiled, the compassion in her expression catching Robert off-guard anew. "Is okay, I help give happy."

Leilani went rigid, head tilted as if to listen. She nodded to herself, bustling toward the kitchen before he could figure out what had happened. He watched her set up at the stove to make...hot chocolate?

Not a moment later, Robert heard footsteps upstairs. He took himself to the kitchen table, out of the way of Cory should the demon come downstairs. Robert listened to the heavy footfalls on the old stairs, eyes trained on the demoness busying herself digging through a cupboard. What was she searching for? Her expression was predatory, the devout intention there banishing the softness she often presented.

Robert shivered. She was even less human than Cory was, but seeing her utter elation at finding her prize still brightened the room. In the nick of time, too, as the hulking demon shambled to the table. He took a seat wordlessly, every action seeming forced and apathetic.

"You'll be all right, bud. Just give it some time."

Cory did not reply, only lifted his hand to inspect the gauze covering where they drew blood. He made to pick at it, scowling at the bandaging in disdain.

Leilani bustled over, her hand finding Cory's to interrupt him, although she never quite touched him, Robert noticed. Instead, she guided the demon's attention to a weathered, antique-looking mug full of steaming cocoa. Like a child mid-tantrum, Cory accepted the distraction slowly, if petulantly. She made to pat his shoulder.

"Don't." It was the first Cory had spoken since his outburst at Kyle, a strained plea for mercy. His expression contorted sharply. "Please."

Leilani nodded, pulling her hand away slowly. Still, he flinched at the movement. "Drink. Have happy, yes?"

Cory nodded, seeming to notice what she had given him for the first time. All at once, Robert watched the demon's apathy melt and crumble to heartbreak. Cory clutched at the mug for dear life, frame buckling beneath the weight of a past Robert could scarcely imagine.

"She has a way of caring for others, doesn't she?" offered Robert as he struggled to smile, if only in reassurance. Things would get better. Cory would get past this, right?

"This was Mom's favorite mug." The demon sniffled and nodded, slowly losing composure as his tears overflowed.

There was nothing to be said anymore. Robert settled in to keep Cory company in the meantime, just the same as Leilani as she sat on the demon's other side. She brought her needlework with her, purring softly as she stitched. It took time, but it helped.

More than Robert could have anticipated, Leilani's inhuman qualities helped Cory. Now more than ever, Robert felt a pit of guilt for considering the small anti-demon Whistle in his pocket necessary.

~~ * ~ * ~ * ~~

It took me a couple of days to come to terms with what happened. How long had I known Cory and he'd never shown that side of himself? How many times had I thought I'd seen him upset, without hearing whatever truly unholy things left his throat that night?

I'm not proud of myself. I managed to gather the courage to come get my things and say goodbye, though. I wasn't entirely sure he even wanted to talk to me, but I owed myself the closure, at least. And, maybe, there was a chance to reconcile. Maybe.

When I approached the farmhouse, it didn't sound like he'd calmed down much from the other night.

"Damn you, what do you want?!" I heard Cory's demand through the kitchen window. The back door opened violently, his voice ringing out more clearly, "I've already lost that chance at human redemption you preach at me about, Charles! What more could you want from me? Just take it! Take it and begone!"

"Don't you dare speak to your grandfather—"

"As though you would weep to be rid of me! Don't speak with that hypocrisy on your tongue," scolded Cory again, and I saw him stalking off to the fields in the back. I abandoned my spot on the front porch, heading around to the kitchen door.

"William, go sit down, you'll strain yourself," I heard Eleanor's gentle words. "Take care of your father, I'll go after him. Both of you just wait here."

I caught up with her where the fields rose up in a wall in front of us. "Eleanor! What happened?"

She turned, breaking into a teary-eyed smile when she saw me. She hugged me tightly. "Oh, Kate! Dear, he said you weren't coming back. Charles commented it was for the better, and Cory...He's so upset, Kate. I haven't seen him have so much trouble in years."

I felt a bit of guilt for having left him to the mercy of his grandfather and thinking he was alone. "I'm sorry, I didn't mean to cause any trouble."

Her smile saddened. "You sound just like him. What can I help you with, Kate? If it's your things, I'm sure—"

"No, I-I'm here for Cory, too, actually," I told her quietly, wringing my hands nervously. She caught sight of that, her motherly hands brushing my arm.

Eleanor looked me in the eye, words firm, "You can find him, then, but be **careful**, Kate. We don't need anyone getting hurt today."

I nodded, shocked she would be so blunt. Was he that bad right now? I tried to imagine what it would be like, after so many years of his having such tight control over himself. He'd let it slip and hadn't been able to regain his footing.

The entire trek through the fields I could hear him, those sounds that belonged in the throat of a bear and not the gentle man we all knew. I'd be lying if I said I wasn't scared. I couldn't shake how he'd looked—fangs bared, eyes cold—like...like a demon. I didn't like the memory, didn't like having the imagery of Cory as anything other than his soft-spoken self. So I pushed on, for the boy I'd always known and the man who deserved more than what he'd been given.

Propped up against a tree, Cory was staring at a photograph he held in one hand, miserable. I could see the tears still on his face, drenching his heartbreak. I'm not sure I'd ever seen him so upset before, over anything. He looked angry and aggrieved at once, too depressed to work up the energy for even his tail to flick about like it normally did.

Something silver glinted in his free hand while I watched and he lifted it to stare at it listlessly. He held it more openly, but it still took me a moment to recognize the flask for what it was. When I did, I gasped quietly, worried. What all had I missed that Cory would be drinking?

"You can come out," he called flatly, still staring at his photo. His brows furrowed, and I could see he was fighting back more tears. "You need not worry, either, I haven't had any yet."

I stepped out of the crops timidly. This was it. I had no clue what to say, but he was waiting for me. When I opened my

47

mouth to speak, nothing came out. I almost felt my heart breaking alongside his, seeing him like this. I was so used to his broad smile, this made me feel like someone had died.

He sighed quietly, gaze softening. "You can return to the house, Mother, I'll be fine. I just need time away, to—"

His words cut off abruptly as he stared at me, first in grief and then in shock. Cory was on his feet in a flash of red, still too surprised to compose himself properly. "Kate. Katelyn, why are you here? If you need your things, I assure you—"

"That's not it," I interrupted him, surprised by myself. My voice was steady and my words sounded much more assured than I felt. "I came by to talk to you about the other night. You sounded upset, so I followed you out here."

"You heard that?" he asked quietly. I nodded, shocked to hear him cursing under his breath in a long string of words I never thought he knew, let alone would say in front of someone. "My apologies, Katelyn. That was...extremely inappropriate of me, and you as a lady—"

"Please stop, Cory," I nearly begged him. I hated how formal he was being with me. It was how he spoke with everyone else, not me. I wanted to be able to walk out and meet him, but I was still shaken from the night of the wedding if I was honest with myself. "You're upset. I understand that, Cory, and I'm willing to work with you on this."

What he was holding fell to the ground as he gaped at me, hope fighting to break free of his carefully crafted mask. "What?"

"I don't want to lose you," I told him honestly, startled by myself. I still hadn't entirely decided until that moment, but what I said was right. The thought of losing him hurt more than I thought possible.

He shook his head slowly, eyes drifting from my face to my bruised legs. "How? What I did..."

I took a deep breath and nodded in agreement, at a loss. What would Jeanine say? "You were...an ass. You were definitely an ass, but something I always forget with you is that nobody's perfect, Cory—not even you, but you sure come close."

"Imperfection is a luxury I can never afford," he replied submissively, clasping his hands behind his back slowly. He was finding his footing, piecing his broken masks together again. "The smallest mistakes on my part—Well, you saw me."

"I did." I crossed my arms over my front protectively. I've never forgotten what that part of him looked like. "But I also know you. You're the man who'd sooner go hungry than see his neighbor go without."

His eyes fell to the ground in shame. "I am more so the animal chained by circumstance."

"You're my best friend." I swallowed thickly. "You've always been my best friend."

*"Kate...I'm sorry. You deserve so much better than this farm," he told me quietly, insisting before I could protest, "You do. You always have. You should go while you can, find some fine young man in the city. Before we repair anything, before you have something you think you can't lose—**please**, Kate," he begged me, stopping me short. All of his dignity, I'd never thought I would ever see Cory genuinely beg for anything, but here he was. "Leave this place."*

He was right. It felt like there was a dagger in my heart, I knew he was so right. I nodded silently, trying to keep myself from crying. "Okay. On one condition."

"Name it," he said too quickly, eager to take care of me even at the cost to himself. I could see how much it hurt him, too. The pain was clear as ever in his eyes.

"Hold me," I told him. That stabbed him, but I couldn't understand why. I only wanted to know if he was still there, the man I cared about. If he wasn't, I could leave. If he was... "Just that, then I can decide."

Cory nodded, forcing a smile for my benefit. "Whatever you desire, my dear."

He held his arms open for me in welcome and I accepted the invitation warmly, wondering what I would do if this really was it, the end. I felt like I should've shattered with the thought of goodbye so near, but Cory's arms held me together, strong and protective around me. One hand rested against my face, his thumb stroking my cheek.

I loved how it felt there, the callouses which made his hands rough with the dedication to his work; the feel of how tender he could be despite his laborer's hands. And how he held me—paying as much attention to me as I was to him. I leaned my head against his chest, closing my eyes as I listened to his heart and felt how much he loved me.

This was him, my Cory, the one I'd wanted to comfort after the wedding. I wish I could say it was happily ever after once I'd finally found him. He deserved that much, to say the least, but it was work. Regaining the trust the one slip had broken, working through the consequences of his lashing out at his family, helping him cope with watching his brother move on to the next stage of life while he lingered like a phantom on the farm.

We tried. That's what's important.

~~ * ~ * ~ * ~~

Robert could not help noticing how much happier Cory had been lately. Since the memorial, if Robert thought it over. If he had to guess, Leilani had something to do with it, too. She had been more friendly than usual with Cory, more confident in her role of helping him. In turn, Cory had been more receptive to her attempts to take care of him. Even now, sitting quietly in the kitchen looking over bills, the demon seemed to have trouble resisting peeking at the woman across the hall.

"You two seem to get along," noted Robert with a smile. His friend started, cheeks deepening to maroon as he caught himself staring at the demoness in the other room. "That's not a bad thing."

"She is a good friend," agreed Cory shyly. He cleared his throat in a nervous habit Robert learned to read years ago. "Strictly a friend, as well."

Robert nodded, unable to fight a smirk. "Getting along usually comes with the territory of being friends, you know."

Cory pursed his lips. "No need to be cute."

"Leilani's got that covered," replied Robert impulsively. He held his hands up in surrender. "Sorry. I meant she's cute in a strictly platonic sense. Like a puppy, or a doll."

The demon hesitated but did not press further. "Katelyn described Leilani as a doll, before...I suppose it fits, in all honesty."

"It's the smile," offered Robert. He was glad to see his friend accept the distraction.

Cory grinned, fangs bared in his good humor. "It is, isn't it? She summons the sun with her smile."

Robert nodded slowly. He would not have described it quite that poetically, but he understood the expression all the same. Leilani certainly was a vibrant woman!

"Of course, that is little compared to her laugh or the lullabies she sings to the children," mused Cory affectionately. His grin faded to a heartfelt smile as he stared at his mug distractedly. "I must find a way to thank her for her presence here."

Robert smiled wide to see his friend focusing on more uplifting topics. "She likes string, but it's also hard to deny the tried and true bouquet."

Cory's expression changed to piqued intrigue. "Perhaps a bouquet of string."

"Ooh, personal, just a little unorthodox but endearing. Exactly the sort of thing women go for," praised Robert. "It's a wonder you're single."

Cory raised one brow skeptically, his silent gesture to his scarred features seeming second nature. "In any case, I will find a way to repay her."

Robert peered into the other room. "I'm pretty sure if you gave her the kids, she'd have to make change with her soul."

"That would defeat the purpose of—My apologies, I seem to have missed your jesting."

"That's all right, it wasn't my best material anyway."

Cory chuckled and nodded, returning his attention to his bills. The distraction did not take, however, the demon glancing back toward the woman in the living room pensively. He hesitated only a second before addressing his companion.

"Robert, I...I lost myself recently," confessed Cory meekly. "She saw it. Leilani saw me, my worst nature, and...Robert, she wasn't afraid of me. I have learned to accept the trepidation of others, but what am I to make of her acceptance when I bare my fangs?"

Robert smiled, guilty to know he had been afraid of his friend before. "Well, what did she do, bud?"

Cory's smile was wistful. "She held me through my grief, bared fangs and all."

~~ * ~ * ~ * ~~

After weeks of waiting, Robert could not contain his excitement when unwrapping the package awaiting him on the counter. Vanessa watched intently, snacking on the grapes cupped in her palm. He tore the shipping envelope open, laughing giddily as a DVD case slid into his hand.

"What's that?"

Robert brandished the case. "Home videos, courtesy of Kate."

She popped a grape in her mouth. "Can I watch?"

"Erm..." He hesitated, realizing through his revelry how it

may be inappropriate. "It's of Cory, from before the Institute. I'm not sure—"

"I'll make popcorn," volunteered Bailey, materializing from the next room. She grinned. "Kate wouldn't give you anything super private, right? It's probably just silly stuff."

Robert had a sudden stab of dread, wondering if there may be mature footage on the disc he held. "Well, I would hope— Girls!"

His daughters giggled, Vanessa making off to the living room with the DVD case as Bailey rushed to toss a bag of popcorn in the microwave. With a defeated sigh, Robert took a moment to pray Katelyn had the sense to only include child-friendly material. What was the worst thing that could turn up on a home video?

Piled on the couch several minutes later, Vanessa sat with the remote on one side of Robert, Bailey with popcorn on the other. The generic DVD selection screen gave way to grainy video. A familiar laugh came over the surround sound.

"Another of your cousin's trinkets, Kate?"

The camera turned its focus on Cory, having to pan up a bit to see his smile. *"How did you know?"*

"Oh, a hunch, given his proclivity for modern technologies."

Kate's giggle was lighthearted. *"Do you have anything you want to tell the future, when this is unearthed by archaeologists?"*

"Mm, never trust a quiet woman." He chuckled and grinned, the frame shaking forcefully. *"Goodness, my dear, no need for violence!"*

The scene cut to a new setting. Robert recognized the interior of the Lawrence home as the camera climbed the stairs, well before they began to protest so adamantly. Katelyn's quiet snicker precluded the door on-screen gliding open to reveal an even more familiar room. On the colossal bed, Cory's figure was splayed out and twisted in the blankets.

Robert had to double-take as the camera drew closer. He had never seen Cory's right arm above the demon's head before!

"Ladies and gentlemen, Mr. Lawrence in all of his unconscious glory!" Kate's whisper was followed by a sound like a boat engine as Cory's unscarred chest expanded. She snorted, audibly choking back a cackle. *"Maybe he'll believe me now when I tell him he snores."*

"Katelyn, must you?" The next scene change was far more abrupt as Cory crossed his arms and stared down the camera. *"There is very little reason for you to be documenting all of this."*

"Oh, Cory dear, I think it's nice," intoned a new voice, motherly in its concern. The frame panned to look at the speaker. Robert's throat felt thick. Eleanor was every bit as kind-looking as Cory said. *"Having a way to look back on the little moments and still hear your voice is something truly remarkable."*

"Is that his mom?" whispered Bailey as the camera panned again. "He talks like her, so she has to be, right?"

"Kate, you're always behind that newfangled contraption," teased an older man, approaching the camera. William? The frame shook, unfocused before Katelyn came into view. *"There we are, now you get to be in the picture, too. How do I capture it?"*

Kate grinned in disbelief and she laughed. *"No, William, it's already—"*

"How's this?"

It cut away to the bedroom again, but the vantage was much different. In the bed, instead of a demon was a small human curled into a ball beneath the covers. A warm chuckle, and the frame lowered as a crimson hand peeled back the covers enough to reveal Katelyn's sleeping face. Using the back of his fingers, Cory stroked her cheek.

"Perhaps now you may see how fortunate I am, my dear,

to have you at my side."

The scene carried on for another minute—Cory continuing his affectionate gesture of caressing her face gently—before it cut back to the DVD menu. Robert scowled, popcorn in hand. Was that it?

"...They really loved each other." Bailey wiped at her cheeks. "I mean, they all really loved him."

On his other side, Vanessa was equally moved. "It's still hard to believe Kate's gone."

"Yeah, it is," agreed Robert quietly. He swallowed thickly. "Well, we've still got popcorn. Would you girls like to find something else to watch?"

Bailey shook her head glumly. "No, thanks. I'm too sad for a movie."

Vanessa released a heavy breath. "I think I'd rather look at my college plans again, if that's okay? I...I want to see if there's anything I can do to help protect Cory and Leilani."

Robert looked between his daughters, taken by their empathy. He nodded. "Okay. That sounds like a good way to spend the evening. Let's do that. Bailey, bring the popcorn."

Herding his daughters upstairs to his study, Robert took a moment to appreciate the evening, simple though it was.

Chapter Three:
Gunpowder

Coming up behind Cory's hunched figure, I peeked at what he was scribbling at so intensely. My sigh of admiration was unintentional, startling us both. His shoulders went rigid, wings stiff in his surprise as he fought a shudder in his tail. He turned his head slowly, managing a look of composure.

"Skulking, Kate?" he accused in his gentle cadence. I smiled, nodding to the picture he'd been working on.

"What's that?"

"Ah." He frowned, lifting the paper to offer us both a better view. "I cannot seem to banish the image from my mind, is all."

"Wow. It...she's...wow." Cory had never been much of an artist, but even his mediocre skills couldn't impair the inherent grace of his subject. It was definitely a she, and she was definitely not human. She didn't look immediately inhuman, though. It was subtle in the shape of her face, the point of her ear. Even the sharpness of her eyes was kind. She didn't look too old, either. Did...had he met someone—like him? "What sparked this?"

He scowled at the paper, frustrated. "I felt compelled, with no reason for it, I'm afraid. Were that I understood the riddle of it..."

I watched how he stared at his depiction of this stranger. He didn't seem too upset by the work itself. In fact, he almost

56

appeared to be enchanted by the forgiving face on the paper. He wasn't hiding something, was he? Would he?

"She looks kind of like a doll," I offered to try and distract from my jealousy. It was only him being creative. He wouldn't be disloyal.

Cory smiled slowly. "I suppose you're right, my dear. Something about her smile?"

"It's her whole face." I gestured broadly at the paper. "Very doll-like."

"Well, now I feel quite foolish, wasting the day away scribbling a doll," he chuckled, setting aside the project absentmindedly. "Now, then, suppose you and I go enjoy the sunset? The honeysuckle is in full bloom and there has been the most pleasant of breezes all afternoon."

"Gonna twist my arm some more, mister?" I teased as I followed him to the front porch's swing. I couldn't shake the picture, though. Something about her made the entire evening feel...stolen.

~~ * ~ * ~ * ~~

"Girls! Breakfast!"

Robert smiled, listening to his daughters as they stampeded downstairs. Anne was setting the table as he brought the serving plate to the dining room. Weekends were quickly becoming his favorite days of the week, now he was spending more time with his family.

"Oh, Bailey, can you—?"

"Morning paper, coming up!"

His youngest bounded out the front door while Vanessa took a seat at the table. "Did you remember the—Ooh, syrup, thank you, Dad!"

"Can't have waffles without it," laughed Robert. Double-checking the placements were ready, he took his own seat for breakfast.

"Dad?!" Bailey's shrill cry from the front door shattered the morning's playful atmosphere. She stumbled into the house, gaping at the newspaper's front page in apparent despair. "Are Cory and Leilani going to be okay?"

As she asked the question, she turned the paper to reveal the main story: Victory for Humans as Demon Sentience Tests Now Mandatory.

Robert blanched, holding one hand out in a silent request. Bailey relinquished the paper, unable to stop her tears as she continued to fret over the implications of the news.

"This won't undo the adoption, will it? I mean, Cory was already independently evaluated as sentient, right? A-and what about Leilani? What if they take her away? What are they planning to do with untested demons, Dad?"

He shook his head slowly, at a loss as he scanned the article. "I'm not sure, sweety, I...I didn't think this would actually pass. I guess, with Kate gone—"

"Is it going to get worse?" wondered Vanessa somberly. She prodded her breakfast with her fork. "For Cory and the others?"

"It's possible. We'll do what we can, but there's only so much—"

"Dad, don't." Vanessa's contradiction was stern, conviction clear. "Kate made a difference."

Bailey sniffled, nodding. "Yeah. She did. We will, too."

~~ * ~ * ~ * ~~

I didn't want to have doubts, but it got harder not to over the years. There were these little things that plain didn't always add up. Cory started to do things that—How could he know something well before it was supposed to happen? Or draw someone he'd never seen, over and over? I'd seen his cuts or bruises heal in a matter of hours.

Once, while he was singing in the fields, I thought I'd watched the crops bloom in response to his voice.

It was too much, especially knowing the side he hid so well. I didn't like to think about it, but maybe he wasn't as much like us as we'd thought. Maybe—

"Paul, do you think Cory's...bad?" I asked quietly. It's not like anyone would overhear when it was just us setting up for the next day's church event.

He did a double-take. "What's brought this on?"

"Well..." I hesitated, thinking of the picture of the girl Cory had drawn. "He's been acting differently. Strangely. He hasn't been sleeping right, I can't explain how, and...things."

Paul looked skeptical. "Things?

"I know how it sounds," I warned him. "It's...not natural, though. He's knowing things before they happen, or healing faster than he should. And he's gotten really good with fire— starting a bonfire in a downpour with two sticks kinds of good."

"Kate." He set one hand on my shoulder to help me focus. His smile was warm as always. "Whatever he is, whatever's happening, it's okay. We don't need to understand what he is when we know who he is."

"I'm scared, Paul." It hurt to admit. "A while ago, I saw the side he hides."

"It's beautiful, isn't it?" He laughed at my expression, clarifying, "It's beautiful that it's taken so long for you to see it, I mean. He doesn't indulge it lightly. In fact, he has always strived to be gentle and approachable. He even seeks extra guidance some mornings, if his work's especially difficult or lonely."

I crossed my arms over my chest, hoping to protect myself from the guilt creeping in. "He visits you?"

"It's a good thing I'm up before dawn anyway," chortled Paul. His concern shadowed his face as he realized I still wasn't comforted. He gave my shoulder a squeeze. "A trick I taught

myself that's helped me, as a pastor, come to terms with having Cory in my flock is thinking of him like gunpowder.

"There's a lot of dangerous applications he could commit himself to, especially where we're concerned. He could raze our town while we slept and no one would be the wiser." Paul's kind *expression softened his description, but I still cringed at the thought because I knew how right he was. "Instead, he recognizes he's dangerous. He puts up safety measures, meters out his slip-ups to keep the whole keg from igniting, and he works harder than most to make something positive of his volatility. Instead of accepting his fate as something destructive, he makes himself fireworks."*

"Oh. Huh."

As out there as his analogy had started, it clicked. He had a point: I'd definitely be more nervous around raw gunpowder than fireworks. It made it easier to look past the oddities cropping up around Cory, too, and just see the good he strove for.

Paul dropped his hand when he saw me relax. "Does that help?"

I nodded. "It really does, thanks. Sounds like you've had to recite that one a lot, too."

His smile was kind, blue eyes sad. "A lot of people are too frightened of the explosion to realize it's just fireworks."

That's stuck with me a long time. Paul had always been one of the kindest men in town. He was probably the first one outside of me or Cory's family to trust him and treat him as a friend. How he made sense of what Cory is helped me with my doubts in so many ways, even if I still get rattled sometimes.

And he was right: a lot of people are too afraid of the explosion to notice it's a firework.

~~ * ~ * ~ * ~~

The barn project was much more extravagant than Robert

had realized. Not only was it a large space, but the facilities seemed a bit excessive simply for horses. Why did each stall have hot and cold running water? Why were there shutters to produce private spaces? The break room was a marvel in its own right, too, with a small locker room—with showers—and what could only be described as a modest cafeteria, complete with buffet line and walk-in food storage. How many employees did Cory intend on having?

Then there was the veterinary clinic. It had a sizable space in the front, rooms in the back for treatment, and a quaint apartment attached. All of this and Cory had still taken the extra step for a fully insulated loft with, again, full amenities?

There was something else going on here, and Robert felt slighted that he was only now realizing the scope of things.

So he turned to the newest residents and first employees of Cory's staff. They had to know something. After all, why else would two specialists in demon medicine accept employment on a *farm*?

"So, you're really going to be working here?"

Bernard looked up from the box he was unpacking. "Huh? Oh, yeah, the big guy called me with an offer I couldn't refuse. No extracurricular, er, *seasoning* in my desserts, but I get to work directly with demons, on-site, with my own apartment *and* an allowance, on top of equipment provided?"

Robert nodded slowly. "That's...good, I take it? I'm not as familiar with your field."

"Pfft, it's amazing! I was packing before I got off the phone with him," scoffed Bernard. He hefted a piece of machinery onto a table. "I'm just honored to be working so closely with demons at all."

"It's rewarding," agreed Robert with a smile. He gestured to the device on the table. "Is that part of the chair you built?"

"This? Yeah, what's left I haven't salvaged, anyway. Terry's been scavenging the corpse for a while." Bernard shrugged, emptying more articles from the box.

"Why break it? That chair was...horrifying, but impressive," praised Robert, hoping the roundabout compliment was taken appropriately.

Bernard paused, confused. "Why? I mean, it worked—which was amazing—but, I don't know, it was pretty invasive. And after some of what we saw, the Institute? I didn't want the wrong hands getting hold of it. So, Terry and I scrapped it, destroyed the programs to run it, and burned the designs. It's not a huge loss, we'll always have more projects to tinker with."

"How was the technology dangerous? You gave me part of it—the Whistle, you called it?"

Bernard froze. "Um, yeah, I did. Because Cory was distressed. Constantly. It was so you could help him if he, I don't know, got lost in the grief? Not self-defense or offense, it—I *can* trust you with it, right? You haven't used it?"

Robert frowned. "That's a very specific use you were hoping for."

"Well, it's not like any psychiatric holds are gonna work on him," laughed Bernard as he pointed out the obvious. "I figured, if you found yourself in that sort of pickle, you'd need the leg-up. Anyway, if he's doing better, you should hide it someplace safe or destroy it."

"Why should I—?"

"You've worked closely with Mr. Lawrence, you shouldn't have to be asking these questions." Terry's voice was quiet but cutting as she finally spoke up from her corner of the room. "Not everyone has the same level of respect for demons. They'd sooner use our inventions as a cattle prod than a medical device. If you're not more mindful of the position demons are in, Mr. Smith, I'm going to have to ask you to not come near our research."

Robert froze in his tracks, abashed, before Bernard stepped in more kindly, "We've been entrusted an incredible opportunity, Robby—not that, Robert, gotcha—anyway, it's an honor to be in this position. Especially after the Institute botched the first contact we've had with demons, possibly ever. Pretend that anything you see us working on can be weaponized against Cory. Because some people will, and most people won't stop them."

His initial curiosity curbed by worry, Robert felt an unsettling chill run down his spine. Something was going on here, and he needed to be mindful not to endanger whatever Cory was hoping to achieve.

~~ * ~ * ~ * ~~

I wish I'd known to appreciate my time with Cory more. I wish I'd known better than to start taking his presence on the farm for granted. If I'd had any idea what would happen to him, I would've committed to living on that farm instead of daydreaming. Or I could've left altogether so he wouldn't feel compelled to risk his safety on my behalf.

I can still hear the gunshots. They never stopped ringing in my ears. Cory's cries of pain, begging for mercy, never stopped, either. There's no describing the pungent smell of demon blood, or how it can feel thick as tar and slick as oil when your hands are drenched in it.

What I remember most is waiting at Paul's, hoping for a miracle, and knowing I was going to be the one to deliver the news of Eleanor's worst nightmares.

I don't know how to describe that phone call.

"...Eleanor?"

"Kate, tell me everything's okay."

I didn't know how to breathe. "Momma, he was shot. Paul says he needs to go to a hospital."

The phone fell on the other end of the line. That didn't matter. I could still hear the scream of denial calling for William.

It was a sound I can never forget. Scuffling on the line startled me.

"Kate, where's Paul taking Cory?" William sounded breathless.

"Ottumwa. I'm going with them, I-I need to—"

"We'll be right behind you, girl. Get him seen to."

William hung up and my attention returned to the blood-stained nightmare of Paul's treatment room. They'd gotten a bullet out, but Cory wasn't his usual crimson anymore. He was this rosy pink which looked plain wrong on him. And he was still muttering.

"...don't-don't let me. I-I-I can't go there. Please, don't let me go there. I can't see the sky...!"

"He's delirious." Paul shook his head, rushing to unstrap Cory from the bed. "Quick, we need to get him into George's van —Kate, bring that stack of blankets!"

The hospital trip was stressful. The next few days were worse, once the media found out about the monster being treated at the hospital. Against faculty approval, as well. Paul was barely allowed to do what he needed, and it was thanks to the support of minor staff Cory was helped at all. We were lucky someone like Paul vouched for him.

I can't remember sleeping. I'm not sure anymore if I did. But I remember just watching Cory in that hospital bed and feeling helpless. Even with Paul advocating for him, Cory couldn't get the blood transfusions he obviously needed: they didn't exist. He had an IV line and was being monitored, meticulously kept at his too-hot temperature with the help of electric blankets. Paul wasn't happy if Cory ever dropped below 105.

When I found out why we'd been out in that storm, the reason he'd been there to be shot, I wasn't sure if I should kiss him or smack him. He could've proposed anywhere and I would've said yes. I felt like I'd failed our relationship if he didn't realize that.

I can still imagine it, the few details we'd discussed for our wedding. He wanted it in the summer when the honeysuckle bloomed, in the sunlight and without the need to hide. It was all he'd ever want, I know, so I suggested using the old tree we spent so many of our afternoons beneath as our alter. One more memory for its old branches to safeguard. He'd wear his suit, I'd wear white, and we would honeymoon on the farm where it was safest.

We didn't have long to celebrate our engagement or his gradual recovery. We were so close to being able to go home. We were almost out of the woods and safe. Just a couple more days and Paul would've had George bring his van to take Cory home.

We almost made it.

And then he was gone.

The farm was empty and cold. Cory's window was barren. His work went undone; crops shriveled without him to sing to them. The smell of him faded from his bedroom. The scores and wounds from his claws faded, worn smooth with time.

~~ * ~ * ~ * ~~

Robert was grateful for the extra amenities of the barn, given he returned the next day to collaborate with the Evans. He had access to information shared by Beth, on top of his own observations, and wanted to give them as much of a head start supporting Cory as possible.

It could help him atone for his past prejudice, he hoped.

A folder rustled softly against the table beside Robert. He looked up from his notes, startled to find Bernard's distressed face, contorted to keep from crying.

"Bernard? What's—"

"Where did you get that folder?" hissed Bernard through

clenched teeth.

Robert hesitated, setting aside his pen to give the doctor his full attention. "It's something I got from Beth, I think. Why? I haven't had time to go through them all."

A sniffle broke through Bernard's control. "Did you know there were others? At the NSISD—there were dozens of subjects."

The blood drained from Robert's face. "I-I thought...Where are they? If they're still in captivity, we should—Bernard, wh-why...what happened to them?"

The doctor shook his head, gesturing defeatedly to the folder. "That's all that's left of them. What was done to them—I don't know how Cory survived it; none of the others did."

"He's always been their prize-winning specimen," muttered Robert bitterly. He glanced at the folder, scowling. "I should—"

"Don't," begged Bernard weakly. "Trust me, Robert, you don't want to see it."

Robert's heart sank. Had he taken action sooner— "...What did they do to him?"

"I'm just glad he's an amnesiac." Bernard shook his head. "You do your job, Robert, and we'll do ours. And if anyone threatens him or another demon with this, we're raising hell."

The doctor grabbed another file from the stacks Robert had to share, stalking off to a corner to continue reading. It was an odd feeling, but Robert found it comforting to know he had allies in the fight for Cory's well-being. After losing Kate, he had felt like a one-man army in a losing battle. He could only imagine how Katelyn had felt all of these years.

Looking around the clinic, already loved by its new doctors, Robert smiled. They may have been later to the fight, but he knew they would never give up ground while they breathed.

Satellites & Shooting Stars

~~ * ~ * ~ * ~~

It took me years to recover from losing Cory. Phone calls weren't enough—not after three years of not knowing. Not after Charlie.

To this day, I'm not sure how I put myself back together enough to start fighting for Cory to be released. I was a single mother, still living in his room as an excuse to cope, but I wasn't ready to give up, and I didn't.

I started petitions. I put out ads. I yelled, I screamed, I raised hell and Hell didn't so much as give me an echo in reply. That is, until someone else who'd been fighting for demons found me. They'd heard of the demon being treated in Ottumwa, then noticed me being loud about Cory's abduction.

Turns out, he'd been piecing together a compound that housed demons in secret, for their own protection. I wanted to know more. I needed to know more, but I didn't even know where to start.

It's not like David King was the best conversationalist, either, but he had more than enough money to speak for him when it came to supporting our mutual cause.

Still, when it came to phone calls I couldn't help glaring at the floor in frustration. "Where are they?"

"Safe." It didn't seem David had any intention of divulging so much as a word more than that in his heavy drawl. "Yer labors are appreciated, Miss Smith."

"Uh-huh," I muttered away from the receiver. I rolled my eyes. "I don't suppose you'll actually be attending the next meeting at the diner?"

He growled. "I don't enjoy public affairs."

"You're awfully reclusive for being our biggest campaign sponsor," I teased. He didn't laugh. If only he could buy himself a sense of humor.

"Bein' reclusive doesn't mean I ain't productive," he

barked back gruffly. He had a point there: his help had gotten us a lot of attention. I didn't enjoy his insisting I be the face of everything, though.

"Don't get your feathers ruffled." It was fun ruffling his feathers, if I'm honest. "Any extra wisdom for us to go over at the meeting, at least? We need to think of the next steps in our campaign, especially when we're ready to take it to the governor."

"Certainly: get yer priorities straight."

I bristled. "Excuse you?"

"You're cryin' to the wrong people, darlin'," rumbled the voice on the line.

I glared at the mail center. "Oh, yeah? How would you know! You're too busy with whatever you do to ignore the issue!"

David sighed patiently. "Where I'm from, we've got a figurehead of sorts, much like all this nonsense you're dealin' with. Thing is, people only follow so long as they can trust 'em to do what's best for everyone."

"And what if they can't? They throw their leaders overboard?" I scoffed and rolled my eyes.

"If a failed leader's lucky? Exile. If they fight back? S'pose that sayin' 'bout bein' eaten alive holds some merit then."

I blanched. I hoped David was joking, but he never joked. He probably didn't know what a joke was to start with. "Oh."

"Yer leaders are failin' to keep everyone safe, darlin'. It's time to get everyone together for an ultimatum."

"That's all well and good to say, Mr. King, but not everyone agrees demons are even people, to begin with."

David laughed. It sounded eerily familiar, but I couldn't figure out why. "You've got the gumption for tacklin' such a problem. They don't see demons as people right now, but you'll make 'em. Come Hell or high water, I know you've got it in you."

~~ * ~ * ~ * ~~

The last several days had been exhausting. Robert had trouble remembering when he last slept—had he at all? Regardless, he was determined to push through his fatigue if it meant helping Cory and the Evans. He was still unclear on what that might be, but the intrigue only fueled his eagerness as he sorted still more notes and files to bring the doctors on his next visit.

"Another mystery file, Beth?" murmured Robert, his empty home office replying with stifling silence. He shuffled through the first pages, pausing to read a note scrawled across the top in vivid red ink.

Should I be unable to help him, you seem an adequate fail-safe.

-Balthazar

Robert frowned. Who was that? One of Beth's colleagues from the Institute? What could possibly need a fail-safe? His questions multiplied, curiosity mounting as he scanned the next page's title. His heart seized before racing off at a panicked gallop.

"Gene therapy?" He flipped through the file anxiously. "Who are all these children?"

The subjects featured each declared history of severe chronic illness, several suspected to have mere months left to their lives. Test groups, Robert realized, for a secret trial of controversial therapy—using Cory's genetic material. Children, *sick* children, being injected with demon genetics.

The trials listed all seemed successful, however. Each subject improved—and then some. Many who were too sick to leave their own home quickly recovered into athletes. There were reports of increased acuity of their senses, as well. Little things which, in Robert's eyes, could bear much more concerning implications.

His cell phone blared abruptly, sending him jumping from his chair as his tightly wound nerves shocked him awake. He gasped a sigh to calm himself, setting aside the folder in exchange for his phone. The caller ID did little to ease his tension as he accepted the call.

"Cory? Is everything okay?"

~~ * ~ * ~ * ~~

I didn't always like David, but his guidance was worth tolerating him. I changed my focus to sway the masses. Richard had already started volunteering his diner—not that he ever spoke more than two words to me when I was there. He was only acting out of a guilt-driven sense of obligation, after all.

Littleton as a whole missed Cory. That was my strong point, and it was what got me an interview on one of Iowa's morning broadcast shows. It was the first big step to getting anywhere, really. Not that I handled the pressure well—I was a nervous wreck hoping I could bluff my way to appearing cool and confident about my cause.

My mistake.

"Can you tell us about your experiences with the Ottumwa creature in question?"

"Yes, he is my fiancé." I couldn't stop anxiously picking at my jeans. It was a good thing Mom couldn't see me doing it, at least.

My host laughed derisively. "Isn't that a little difficult, having a relationship with an animal?"

"No. He isn't an animal. His name is Cory Charles Lawrence, and he is one of the best men I've ever known," I replied sharply.

He wasn't listening. Judging by his continued laughter, he wasn't taking me seriously, either. "What's it like, being with an animal? Those claws look dangerous!"

"His name is Cory," I pressed stubbornly. "He keeps a journal. He'd never stop reading if he had the chance, and I don't think I've ever seen anyone wear down a record the way he does when he finds the right sound. His name is Cory."

"I didn't know you could train demons to read or write! Does it need supervision, or—?"

"His name is Cory. Say it."

"Come on, now, don't get mad—Oh, we've got a caller! You're on the air, watcha got?"

There was a moment of static before a familiar voice spoke up, and I felt like I could scream. "His name's Cory, and it's not right for you to be treating his girl this way, either."

My host faltered for a second, laughing nervously. "Heh, who's this? Someone she paid to step in? Are you pranking us?"

"Look, you aren't cute, it isn't witty or funny, or whatever it is you're trying to be," said Richard sternly. "His name's Cory. He's a good man and she's just trying to get help bringing him home. Show some respect."

The line disconnected, but I got the feeling Richard wasn't done scolding yet. My host plain didn't want to hear it anymore. "That's all for that, now let's—aaand we have another caller! You're live! What's your input about this demon—?"

"His name is Cory. That boy's done plenty and worked hard for his community. Get it right."

I couldn't place the voice immediately. It had to be one of the other farmers Cory had helped over the years. He'd been quiet, keeping his head down and doing what needed done for anyone who asked for help. I couldn't believe anyone was standing up for him.

"It's not funny anymore. Who is this?"

"Doesn't matter. Get his name right."

And on, and on, and on. Even Paul called in to chastise

the host mocking Littleton's lost citizen. Heartbreaking as it was, the biggest push we had was when Eleanor called in.

"I don't know who's listening, but please, help us bring my son home."

It worked. We caught the public's eye. People were paying attention. Suddenly, the demons attacking weren't mere animals, they were people acting in self-defense and in need of advocacy. We had the momentum we needed to start making demands for Cory's release. Rights were a long ways off, but if we could have him come home on any kind of probation we'd take it.

Too little, too late.

Out of the blue, Cory stopped calling. Paul wouldn't talk about it. We assumed the worst, and the NSISD refused to give us any closure. No one would tell us if he was alive; no one would release his body if he had passed. It was over.

We had the funeral, and I moved away from Littleton. Away from the memories, away from the reminders of loss. I was done. I only wanted to focus on raising Charlie, and Jeanine and her husband helped me. Richard stepped up and put her through college—one more apology. He got damn good at those. I even started looking forward to visiting him for the annual memorial.

What we'd built together didn't stop, either. David kept going, more people stepped in, and before I knew it you were reaching out to me. Not only to congratulate me on my efforts to secure demon rights, but to seek my guidance on the NSISD's sole living specimen. I'd lost my daughter, my health, my hope for seeing my grand-babies' futures be bright. You gave me back my fireworks.

Thank you, Robert.

~~ * ~ * ~ * ~~

The door opened before Robert could knock. He was

greeted by Leilani's fanged grin. The expression was nothing short of welcoming, far from the mortifying, predatory display he had first believed it to be. Instead of shivering in fear, he returned the expression with a smile.

"Robert!"

"Hi, Leilani." He laughed at her enthusiasm when she flung open the door to invite him inside. "You look chipper, as always. Is Cory in the house or out back?"

The demoness paused as she closed the door behind Robert. "Cory? Oh! Cory! Cory, see Robert! Come!"

"Come in, Robert, make yourself at home," called Cory from the kitchen. As Robert made his way into what was arguably the heart of the Lawrence home, he faltered. "Ah, yes, erm...I felt the occasion may require being fortified with a hearty supper."

"Hearty...?" echoed Robert in surprise, gaping at the spread.

Cory chuckled nervously, removing the too-small apron he wore. "I, ah, may have also picked up Mother's habit of cooking to calm the nerves."

"Well, I'm here, so let's get you a break, bud. Come on, what's on your mind?"

As they each took a seat at the table, the demon released a weighted sigh of relief. "Very well. I suppose I should confess, I feel as though I may have bitten off a mite more than I can chew."

Robert frowned. "In a good way or...?"

Cory chuckled again, even more nervously. "I, ah...yes, I would say so. Even with the work of packing away the last of Kate's effects."

"Do you need a hand with anything?" asked Robert after a moment to watch his friend's sorrowful expression.

The demon forced a smile. "No, but thank you. I've nearly finished with it. Ah, and there seems to have been something for you, as well. My apologies for the poor timeliness of its delivery."

"You're feeling better, though?" wondered Robert, tucking away the letter being offered without so much as a second glance.

Cory took a deep breath as he considered his answer. "Yes. The year has been trying, make no mistake, but...I finally feel as though there is clarity in the future."

Robert smiled, relieved to hear his friend was doing so well. "That's good, bud. How about the kids? Still shaken up?"

"That *stunt* their father pulled caused quite the stir in our home," growled Cory, visibly having difficulty maintaining his meticulously choreographed expression. "We've come through the other side stronger, though. The children's nightmares have eased again, and they seem more confident in their relationship with Leilani and I. Silver linings, I suppose."

"It's good to look on the bright side." Robert frowned. "If things are going so well, though—I'm sorry, I'm just confused, you sounded urgent over the phone. Did something else happen?"

Cory hesitated. "Ah. Well, yes, Robert, there is something I would appreciate your insight on. Or, rather, a trusted voice to help me steady my thoughts on the matter."

Robert shrugged, his reply interrupted by an aggressive knock on the front door. He frowned. Who else could be coming to the Lawrence house at this time of night?

Cory blanched, taking a deep breath to steady himself. His composure came quickly, slipping into his most approachable mask as he stood to answer the door with a polite smile.

"Henrickson. To what pleasure do I owe your team the visit?"

Satellites & Shooting Stars

Robert,

I hope this gets to you, somehow. If I make it home to give it to my lawyer, or...maybe it'll be found later, if I don't. I need to believe in the best right now, though.

I've seen them, the demons, the sides of Cory he keeps so bottled up inside. They're terrifying, Robert. Like wild animals, except they talk and smile and laugh—they're animals, but they've only expressed curiosity and concern for me and my grand-babies. I've seen them snap branches like twigs, or prepare an animal for a roasting spit without so much as a knife to skin it.

They're animals. The few I've been able to talk to makes me think they weren't always like this. I've heard fragments of their culture and history; I wish I could've seen it. The stories I've heard make them sound like people, and amazing ones. They have a history.

As terrifying as the demons are, there's something much, much worse in Paradise: angels. I've been wondering what the demons did wrong to provoke a war, Robert, until...She's this tiny thing and reminds me of a doll. The girl Cory drew when he was younger, I met her here, Leilani? She talks at me. I don't have a clue what she's saying, but I know she wouldn't hurt a fly to save her life. She couldn't have done anything to deserve the baggage I can see her carrying.

Nothing could have deserved how they've been stripped down, piece by piece, from proud people to this fractured culture, struggling to recover. They're trying. They deserve the chance to be built up and thrive again.

Cory wants to help them. Let him. Encourage him. Enable him. Please. Make sure that my grand-babies are safe and Cory gets home to them at the end of the day. He needs to know where he comes from and he needs to accept how terrifyingly, breathtakingly otherworldly the people he comes from can be. Just be there for him while he learns how to smile without hiding his fangs, okay?

And, if you're the friend I think you are, while you stick around, be careful. Accidents happen, but most importantly— don't fear what the demons are right now, fear the things that curated it.

More titles by Karma Rose:

Demon Rising
Broken Orbit
Cinderella Dances

In *Angel Falling,*
Cory finds himself trapped
as the angels close in.

After *Broken Orbit* saw drastic changes to his life, Cory Charles Lawrence now finds himself harboring demons in his barn. Torn between worlds—too human for his nature, too inhuman for his culture—unable to find purchase in either. As he struggles to balance the duality of who and what he is, angels draw nearer from without while something sinister stirs inside his skin.

Can he keep his family safe?

And how far will he go to help his own kind despite their rejection?

Coming October 15th, 2021

__Prologue__

Robert Smith was beyond appalled by this.

"What are you people doing?! Hey! What gives you the right?!" Lisa was voicing her own concerns, and as the soldiers continued through the house in such a ransacking fashion Robert considered joining in her protests.

"Let them do their jobs," intoned Cory calmly, linking his hands behind his back. He was standing to the side patiently, his kids beside him, while his home was being turned upside down. The intrusion was unwelcome and unanticipated, to say the least.

"I understand you know these guys, but...Cory, you really don't have to put up with this," interjected Robert nervously. What were they even searching for?! Could it have anything to do with why Cory had called him out here so urgently? "You have rights!"

"What is *this*?" came the gruff demand of Santos. The man was obviously struggling with his own moral quandary about the situation as he dragged Leilani down the stairs by the arm. Even standing equal to her assailant's height, the coral little demoness was far from intimidating, whimpering meekly as she was tugged roughly along.

"That?" Cory nodded to the woman, keeping his expression reserved and cool. He smiled politely and raised one brow. "My nanny dog, more or less. No worries, I have her trained for polite company as well as tagged in the event she is brought off-property. You may check her collar, if need be."

Santos fought a cringe as he reached for Leilani's throat and the brand-new leather dog collar there. He found the metal tag, reading the information etched into it before nodding and passing her off to the larger demon. "Good. Can't have wild demons running around loose, you know."

Cory nodded with painfully quiet understanding. "Of course not, sir."

All the while, Lisa was huffing indignantly and Robert could do nothing to oppose this blatant disregard of civil rights. As the soldiers finished upending the home's interior, they made for the back door. Robert overheard them mentioning the barn, to which Cory's attention was more than rapt.

"Excuse me, gentlemen, but I have expensive equipment in the barn. May I accompany you to ensure its safe handling?" he requested politely, following after them as Santos nodded. There was still reluctant detachment, although that was quickly melting away as they fell back into their cordial familiarity. "Thank you, I appreciate the consideration."

Robert and Lisa followed close behind while Leilani huddled in the living room with her charges, murmuring comforts to their confused, distressed questions. The soldiers had difficulty keeping pace with Cory as he strode briskly to the barn. He wore a calculating expression that Robert found chilling. He was so accustomed to his friend being warm and inviting; this stern nature was something entirely new.

Henrickson and Santos were the soldiers to accompany the demon into the building, leaving Thompson and two others to watch the fields. As Robert entered shortly behind, he overheard some of the hushed conversation within.

"...is a violation of the new laws, Cory, what the hell?!" Santos was stunned and overwhelmed.

"Please, both of you, this is...a rescue, of displaced exotic animals. I swear to you, they will be documented and registered shortly," replied Cory urgently. Robert watched the men on the other end of the large barn, unable to move through the shock of it all.

The barn was huge, but he had seen that already. What he had not realized was that every stall was occupied now, demons huddled in their confines and terrified by the abrupt intrusion. The air was stale, tension palpable as even Robert could taste the fear.

When had this happened? He peered into the nearest stall, recognizing Braxen standing in the far corner. The bull demon was glowering hatefully at the stall door, fangs bared in a silent snarl. The expression sent a shiver of terror through Robert, and he had to resist the urge to yelp when the demon turned his harsh violet eyes on him. His blood went cold. Cory had never looked at him like this before. No, his friend had always been so very well-mannered and in control of his appearance to others. This demon was...wild—untamed and angry.

"Santos is right, Cory, this is something we can't overlook." Henrickson was talking now, subdued and regretful. Robert had never heard the man speak so emotionally before. "There's too many of them to go unnoticed. A single little one with a collar is one thing, but this..."

"Please, Henrickson." Cory reached out and gripped the man's shoulder firmly. "You know as well as I that this...this is not right. I will abide by the law, I only need the time to mark them as domesticated animals. Please. I will keep them as hidden as I can until then, you have my word."

Henrickson was quiet, the tension in the barn growing further, but Robert could not peel his eyes away from Braxen's loathing stare. "Exotic breeding stock. I'll see if we can buy you time, but I can't promise much. There were too many eyewitness accounts in the area to delay investigation more than a couple weeks. Tops."

"Thank you, sir. I will begin as soon as possible, these people—*animals*...They need to settle before I stress them more." The relief in Cory's voice melted to shame quickly. "Thank you."

"Hmph." There was a quiet moment, and Braxen's glare flicked to the door again, his head tilting to the side inquisitively as he listened as intently as Robert did. "What's that, then?"

"Staff quarters and our on-site veterinary room," replied Cory candidly. He sounded proud, as though his stalls truly were housing champion-bred horses. "You are more than welcome to investigate. Our facilities are up to standard, and we have all of the appropriate licensing for staff and facilities alike."

Santos swore fluidly in a foreign language. "Cory, what are you doing? You could end up in prison again, or worse."

"There are few things worse than neglecting morality for the sake of ease," replied the demon grimly. "It is all I have to show as being human, and I will not disregard it lightly."

"Come on, Santos, there's nothing but some breeding stock and equipment in here. The property is clean," barked Henrickson, and the men made their way back toward where Robert was barely gaining his confidence enough to step away from Braxen's stall.

"Hey, shrink, long time," acknowledged Santos as he strode past and out of the barn. Henrickson followed close behind, barking orders to the men outside while Cory lingered behind.

The hulking demon sighed shakily, the weight of the situation leaving him in a visible rush. "Oh, that was...unpleasant."

"What are you going to do, Cory?!" whispered Robert furiously. He gestured to the huge lane of stalls. "Is this what you had planned all along?! I thought you were going to go into livestock!"

"Convincing, isn't it?" chuckled Cory darkly. His emerald eyes were still perturbed, even as he smiled invitingly to his friend. "I have a plan, Robert. These people will be safe here."

"How?! A hundred collars?! And what happens if those get lost!" he hissed viciously. This was absurd!

The demon's expression only saddened, an odd guilt settling into the set of his brow. "No, Robert, that would be ridiculous. They *are* livestock, after all. You don't collar cattle."

For a light love story,
pick up *Cinderella Dances*

Apathetic spinal surgeon Dr. Li feels drawn to an almost stranger: Elaine Crowley. When he recognizes her in his operating room, he realizes he will stop at nothing to help her dance again.

In this modern retelling of Cinderella, Prince Charming stand-in Doctor Da Li is well out of his element as he discovers a connection to our pauper princess Elaine.

Available now

<u>Accidents Happen</u>

None of this was supposed to happen.
The thought possessed me, body and soul, as I took in the face of the woman lying there. The first thing I could feel was glad—glad that she wasn't awake to recognize me. Not because I knew her so well or some other drama. My reason was far more mundane because, truthfully, I knew so little of this woman. What disquieted me was how well she knew me—five minutes a day, five days a week, for the last three months, and she knew more of my habits than most of my coworkers.

She worked at the chicken place nearest my hospital. I stopped by for lunch each day, and she always took my order. It was a fact of life I had acknowledged nearly two months ago when she had my order cooking before I walked in and bagged by the time I reached the front of the line.

I should have known something was wrong when she wasn't there today, but I hadn't thought about it. I didn't even know her name, yet now I was staring her bruised, damaged body in the face with nothing to say, no way to compensate.

"Doctor? Doctor!" My assistant caught my attention abruptly, startling me back to reality. "We need to operate immediately."

I nodded once, determination settling in where my guilt had taken residence. "Of course. Ready the operating room."

~~ * ~ * ~ * ~~

"How's your cat?"
"I'm sorry?"
The woman smiled. "Your cat. You said that she had an infection and you were worried about her, last week. How is she?"

I had stopped where I was, shocked by the fact that she had remembered when I couldn't even recall telling her. But that was just a memory now, a ghost of the girl who could stand. Now, I had to look all of that kindness in the eye and deliver the bad news.

When she saw me walk into the room she smiled, a strangely heart-wrenching sight after her accident. "Doctor. I never thought I'd be seeing you here."

I attempted to return the smile, no matter how strained it may be. "Well, you weren't at the restaurant, Miss Crowley, so I decided to come here for lunch."

She laughed quietly at me, and I could see how worried she was becoming. "So, Doctor Li. What happened? Why am I here?"

This I could do, this I could say. I had delivered very similar news countless times before. "You were in an accident, walking to work. Your head hit the pavement rather hard, so it's expected if you have difficulty with your recollection of the event."

She nodded slowly, a look of dread contorting her expression. "Okay. What else? Why can't I feel my legs? Doctor Li? Doctor?"

There it was again, that guilt. *She shouldn't be here.* "Where the car hit you—There's damage to your lower spine. We operated immediately, to do what we could, but...We won't know anything for certain for several weeks, at least."

"You mean I might never walk again?" she choked on her words, the sound wrenching the heart in my chest. I'd given the same news dozens of times before. This time shouldn't have been any different.

But my eyes refused to meet hers as I nodded. "It is a possibility, but there is a chance that, with treatment and physical therapy, in a couple of years..."

"In a couple of years, I won't have a job. Or a home," she replied faintly, trying so hard to be brave, I could see it. Every day for the last three months, she had helped me without even a sincere thanks to take home. Now, when there was the opportunity to return her efforts, I didn't know how; I'd never cared enough to learn.

"I'm sorry," was all I could think to reply with, loathing how the seconds dragged by in agonizing silence. "If you need anything, please don't hesitate to call the nurse. She'll help to make you as comfortable as possible."

With that, I turned to leave, at once grateful and regretful that there was nothing left to say. No way to help and no way to lie anymore about the severity of her condition. Nothing to do but move on.

"Wait!" Her outcry stopped me short, and I was glad for it, though I didn't look back at her. "Thank you."

I winced at the words, but I was far from any mood to interpret my reactions at this point. I nodded curtly. "You're welcome."

~~ * ~ * ~ * ~~

Three days.

That was all, but I still couldn't seem to get away from that woman, Elaine. Months after first meeting her, I finally knew her name and now I couldn't get it out of my head.

"Hey, Li, you all right? Your head doesn't seem to be in the game today." Mark brought my attention back to the game of chess we were engaged in like we did every Saturday morning. Doctor Hart was a colleague of mine. Having met in college, we'd remained close friends since.

I took in the game and, with a quiet sigh, brought my knight to check. "What do you mean? I'm going to win."

He made a narrow escape by sacrificing a bishop, nodding. "But you usually beat me a lot sooner. If I didn't know better, I'd say I almost had a fighting chance."

That made me smile. "But you still know better, Mark."

"Okay. How about a bargain? I win, you tell me what's bothering you," he continued persistently.

"And what if I win?" I captured the sacrificial bishop, one move closer to victory.

"I'll spring for dinner," was his immediate reply, moving forward a pawn rather than defending his king.

"I'm agreeable." My knight moved forward. "Check."

His queen struck from nowhere, throwing me off guard. Mark grinned. "Checkmate."

I stared at the setup, taking it in slowly, praying there was a way out. "Of all the times for you to improve..."

"So." He leaned back with a triumphant smile. "Who is she?"

"What?" I stared at him in shock. "That is a rather bold assumption."

"Well, it was that or drugs," he replied offhandedly. "So, again, who is she?"

I sighed quietly in defeat, shaking my head slowly. "I should have known you never would have bought me dinner."

He smiled patiently. "I'm waiting, Li."

"I never agreed to a time frame."

"No, but you still agreed," he pointed out with a smug smirk.

I nodded slowly, weighing my options. After all, guilt aside, there was no need to be unnerved by anything to do with Elaine. She was simply another unfortunate patient that I happened to recognize. Nothing more.

"All right. One of my patients—"

"Oh, *really*?!"

"—I just recognize her, that's all," I finished firmly, not wanting him to get the wrong idea. "Honestly, I may just be tired, she may have nothing at all to do with this. We *have* been busy," I added for extra effect. My efforts were met with a disbelieving scowl.

"You've gone seventy-two hours without sleep and still never lost to me before," he countered earnestly. "I'd like to know: Is she pretty? I mean, what kind of girl catches the eye of the great and stoic Doctor Li?"

I shot him a glare. "One who isn't my patient, Mark."

"So, we only have a few weeks to find out, then, huh?" He shrugged. "I can wait."

"Please, Mark, spare me. You're coming dangerously close to sounding perverted," I threatened him. Much to my dismay, it seemed to have very little effect on him.

"Takes one to know one, but you're getting away from the topic of interest." He stared me in the eye and asked, "Who is she?"

About the Author

Karma Rose was an unschooled student and has always been a writer at heart. Although she began with poems and short stories, she has now since completed two installments in her *Gravity* series, *Demon Rising* and its sequel, *Broken Orbit*. She spends her days tending her small farm.

For updates on current and future projects, look for Karma Rose on various social media platforms or interact directly at Ko-fi.com/karmarose!